Got To Be Love

Book 3

Loving You Series

By:

Vanessa Miller

Got To Be Love

Vanessa
Miller

Book 3
Loving You Series

Vanessa Miller

www.vanessamiller.com

Printed in the United States of America

© 2019 by Vanessa Miller

Praise Unlimited Enterprises
Charlotte, NC

Other Books by Vanessa Miller

Family Business I

Family Business II

Family Business III

Family Business IV

Family Business V

Family Business VI

Our Love

For Your Love

Got To Be Love

Rain in the Promised Land

Heaven Sent

Sunshine And Rain

After the Rain

How Sweet The Sound

Heirs of Rebellion

Feels Like Heaven

Heaven on Earth

The Best of All

Better for Us

Her Good Thing

Long Time Coming

A Promise of Forever Love

A Love for Tomorrow

Yesterday's Promise

Forgotten

Forgiven

Forsaken

Rain for Christmas (Novella)

Through the Storm
Rain Storm
Latter Rain
Abundant Rain
Former Rain

Anthologies (Editor)
Keeping the Faith
Have A Little Faith
This Far by Faith

Novella

Love Isn't Enough
A Mighty Love
The Blessed One (Blessed and Highly Favored series)
The Wild One (Blessed and Highly Favored Series)
The Preacher's Choice (Blessed and Highly Favored Series)
The Politician's Wife (Blessed and Highly Favored Series)
The Playboy's Redemption (Blessed and Highly Favored Series)
Tears Fall at Night (Praise Him Anyhow Series)
Joy Comes in the Morning (Praise Him Anyhow Series)
A Forever Kind of Love (Praise Him Anyhow Series)
Ramsey's Praise (Praise Him Anyhow Series)
Escape to Love (Praise Him Anyhow Series)
Praise For Christmas (Praise Him Anyhow Series)
His Love Walk (Praise Him Anyhow Series)
Could This Be Love (Praise Him Anyhow Series)
Song of Praise (Praise Him Anyhow Series)

Dedicated to:

My cousin Carol Underwood (Gone to soon)

Prologue

The pain was excruciating, he had never gone this far before. But the doctor confirmed that Gina had a broken arm and cracked ribs. Marvel Williams had told her that he loved her and wanted to marry her.

The nurse put a cast on her arm and then left the room as a police officer who looked like he'd just barely graduated high school stepped into the room. He was so thin, a strong wind could blow him over. Gina doubted that this man, whether police officer or not, could protect her. So, when he asked, "Who did this to you?

She said, "I fell."

"Ma'am, your injuries aren't consistent with a fall. Tell me the truth so we can help you."

But she couldn't tell him, or something bad would happen to her, Marvel promised he'd kill her, and she believed him. He was violent and vicious. She hated him, wished him nothing but the worst. But she couldn't file a complaint because she was terrified that he would make good on his threats.

How things had turned so bad, Gina didn't know or understand. She had just received a promotion and took Marvel out to celebrate.

Some guy looked at her a moment too long and everything got crazy from there. Marvel told her, "You got that promotion and now you think you can stare at other men right in my face?"

No, not again, she thought. She just wanted to enjoy an evening out with her man. She didn't want to make Marvel mad. She didn't need nor want this kind of drama in her life. "I wasn't looking at anyone. I was just sitting here talking to you."

Pushing his chair back, he stood, threw a few dollars on the table and said, "Come on, let's go."

"Please don't get upset Marvel, let's just have some fun tonight, okay?"

He grabbed her arm and snatched her out of her seat, "I said let's go."

"Are you sure you don't want to tell the police what happened," the nurse asked after the officer left the room.

Her nurse was an older woman with gray hair and kind eyes. She reminded Gina of her grandmother. She desperately wanted to tell someone about what she was going through. But she didn't see a way out, so there was no use.

"Can I pray with you?" The nurse asked.

Prayer. She'd done a lot of that as a teenager in youth ministry at her church back in Detroit, Michigan. But during college, she hadn't had much time for God or youth ministry. After college, she met Marvel, and he wasn't a churchgoer, so Gina hadn't thought much about going to church either.

Now she was in trouble and she needed God like she never needed Him before. As tears fell down her face, she said, "Please pray for me."

The nurse bowed her head as she held onto Gina's hand, the hand that didn't have the cast on it. "Lord, I come to you on behalf of this beautiful young lady. Lord, we know that You are a good God and You desire good things for us. So, I ask that you first help Gina to see the joy that comes with serving You so You can save her soul. I also ask that You lead and guide her away from all hurt, harm and danger. That includes any relationship that might be bad for her. Make a way of escape for her, Lord Jesus."

The prayer sparked a fire in Gina because it finally helped her to realize that she could escape. She just needed the Lord to show her the way.

1

Looking out the window, Gina Melson could hardly believe that the sun was shining so bright in the midwest on December 28th. It was a beautiful day for a wedding, coupled with the fact that it was still the Christmas season, so the wedding was going to be festive. Gina was excited to be a bridesmaid at her best friend's wedding. The only issue she had was that her car was not in the driveway where she left it last night. Frantic and about to call 911 to report her bright red BMW stolen, Gina then remembered the conversation she had with the bank thirty days ago.

She had been sixty days past due on the BMW at that time. They demanded their money or the key. Business had been slow, and Gina had barely been getting by. Her pantry had Ramen noodles in it, something she swore she'd never eat again after college. Her heat was even set at 68 degrees, she now had a cold and had worn out her favorite fluffy pink socks.

No matter how many adjustments she made, the money still wasn't flowing like it had when she was climbing the ladder at her old PR firm. Gina blamed Marvel Williams for all her woes. He claimed to love her, but Marvel didn't have love in his heart for anyone but himself. After breaking her arm, he belittled and terrorized her until she quit a job she loved so she could move out of the country to get away from him.

Gina used up a great deal of her savings while living in the Bahamas and basically hiding out from her abuser. When she did move back to the United States, she moved into an upscale condo division that had security. Gina was just beginning her PR firm and couldn't afford the condo, but she needed to feel safe.

Rolling her eyes at her current situation, she tried to use her cell phone to arrange an Uber pick up but the call was redirected to Sprint. Her phone had been cut off for non-payment. Gina made arrangements to pay the bill in two weeks and they reconnected her service. Where she would get that money in two weeks, Gina didn't know.

But once her phone was reconnected, she called her mom. She hadn't told her parents about her financial woes, but it couldn't be helped now. She didn't want to spend extra money on Uber when she had just made an arrangement to pay a past due cell phone bill. "I need your help, Mom."

"I'm getting ready for the wedding but let me know what I can do."

Her mom was always so accommodating, and Gina loved her for it. "I need a ride to church."

"Don't tell me that fabulous BMW of yours broke down?"

Gina hated admitting the truth but lying was not an option. She believed the words of the Bible that said a liar can't tarry in God's eyesight. So, she refused to make up lies when the truth was readily available. "I'm behind on payments so they repossessed it."

"Oh, my goodness. Do you need money?" Audrey Melson asked her daughter.

"No, Mom, I'm handling it. I just need a ride."

"Okay, hon, I'm on my way."

"Thank you." Gina hung up and waited on her mom to pick her up as if she was sixteen again, staying after school for cheerleading practice and then needed to wait on her ride to get home. Her mom picked her up and drove her to the church so she could perform her duties as a bridesmaid and that was all she really cared about right now.

Three days after Christmas, Gina would have thought that people would be off work, still enjoying the Christmas spirit and spending time with their families. But evidently, the taxman and collections departments don't close for Jesus, family, or nobody else. Gina was at her breaking point. But she had thoroughly, no-turning-back-this-time given her life to Jesus about six months ago, so she turned to Him as she sat in the passenger seat of her mother's Toyota Camry. Gina bowed her head and silently prayed, "Lord, I trust You. Things are shaking right now. I don't know what to do to get over this hump. Please help me. I need a financial breakthrough, not tomorrow or next week, but today."

"Tell Mama what's going on. How can I help you, hon?" Her mom asked while putting a hand on Gina's shoulder for comfort.

The last thing Gina wanted to do was burden her parents. They were retired and just barely getting by on the pensions they thought would carry them through. "It will be alright, Mom. Being my chauffeur is a tremendous help to me. And you drive around listening to praise music. What?" Gina turned up the radio and started rocking to *Can't Nobody Do Me Like Jesus* by Maranatha Gospel.

Popping her fingers and steady rocking, Gina said, "What that man say, Mama?"

"I hear him… can't nobody do you like Jesus, so you want your Mama to step back." Audrey nodded, understanding her limitations now that her daughter was a full-grown woman.

Gina exhaled as they pulled up to Christ-Life Sanctuary. She was truly enjoying the praise music and it was encouraging her soul. But in truth, she'd only turned up the volume to get her mother to think about Jesus rather than her daughter's problems.

They got out of the car and Gina's mother looped her arm around her arm. "Trouble don't last always," Audrey said to Gina as they entered the church.

Before the weariness she was feeling could set in, Gina activated her faith and pointed heavenward." It can't last forever, because we belong to Him."

Audrey brought Gina's head to her shoulder as she laid a kiss on her forehead. "I'm so thankful to God that you came back home."

"Me too, Mama." She left her mother in the entryway and went to the back of the church, where the bridal party was using the prayer room to get dressed.

"You made it." Toya Milner opened her arms for a hug as she sat at the table, having lash extensions added to her eyelashes.

Gina rushed to her best friend and hugged her. "Of course, I made it. I wouldn't miss your big day for anything."

"Help!" Toya called out.

"What's wrong?" Gina stepped back. "Was I hugging you too tight?"

"I can't open my eyes."

The best laugh she'd had all week occurred while watching Toya try to open her eyes as the glue from the eyelash extensions on the top eyelid connected with the bottom lid and stuck together.

Toya's eyelashes fluttered; the glue still wouldn't give. Then the make-up artist started flaring her arms like she was coming in for a landing, "I told you not to blink. Didn't I tell you?"

"How can I avoid blinking? Eyes blink. That's what they do." Toya kept struggling to open her eyes.

The make-up artist worked on the lashes, trying to pull them apart and Gina grabbed her belly as she doubled over laughing. "I'm sorry, I'm sorry. I know this shouldn't be so funny to me, but I need this laugh today."

"And I need my eyes to stay open so I can walk down the aisle and marry my man." Toya widened her eyes, trying to keep the lashes from touching again.

Gina wanted to stop laughing but Toya looked so silly while holding her eyes open like that. The make-up artist didn't help the situation as she stood in front of Toya with a mini fan on high. Blowing hot breath in Toya's face. "Men will never understand what we women go through to be beautiful and glamorous."

"Tia, Toya's younger sister agreed. "And all they have to do is shave and throw on their clothes, then stand there complaining about how slow we are."

Gina then told Toya, "Next time get the strip lashes. Those individual lashes are more pain than they are worth."

"Tia talked me into it." Toya pointed toward her very pregnant sister.

"Don't blame me." Tia held onto her stomach as she struggled to stand and waddle over to her sister. "I can't be held responsible for anything I say or do until this baby comes out."

"How much longer," Gina asked.

"Three more weeks."

"Looks like you ready to pop today. Don't let your water break and get all over my shoes while we're standing at the altar." Gina glanced down at her gray Manolo Blahnik's. They were the most expensive pair of shoes she owned other than a pair of glittery Jimmy Choo's that she normally brought out on New Year's Eve. But she would probably be selling her precious shoes at a second time around shop if things didn't turn around quickly. Probably should have gotten rid of them a long time ago anyway since they had been gifts from her evil ex. But most women would have agreed with her decision... get rid of the man, keep the shoes.

~~~

David Pittman pulled up to the church and was about to get out of his car when the phone rang. He wouldn't have answered, but it was his business manager, they were finalizing the paperwork on the deal with the Foodie Network channel. "Katie, my lady, whatcha know good?" Katie had been his business manager for three years. There had never been anything romantic between them, but he always said that silly rhyme when answering her calls.

"Doubt you'll consider what I have to say good news."

"Wrong answer, Katie. I don't want to hear any bad news. Everything was supposed to be wrapped up with the network this week."

"They're a little worried about recent developments."

David was so frustrated, he wanted to punch something. "This is bogus!" He shouted into the phone as if the utterance of those words would make a difference.

"I know that, David. I'm on your side. We just have to get the people who matter to see the real you."

"Easier said than done." David shook his head. "Look, I've got to go. I'll get back with you tomorrow."

15

"But I need you back at the office. We've got an emergency situation here. We need to brainstorm and figure something out before we lose this contract."

"I hear you. But I made a promise to my college roommate, I need to be right where I'm at. I'll get back with you." He hung up the phone as he tried to push the multi-million dollar deal that was on the verge of collapsing out of his mind, he got out of the car and walked into the church to fulfill his duty as best man to an old friend.

2

Toya's eyelashes finally dried, she was a beautiful bride as she walked down the aisle with Thomas Reed by her side. Toya's father passed away five years ago and her mother, Yvonne, married Thomas, who was Jarrod's father, about two years ago, they now pastored Christ Life Sanctuary church together.

Gina nudged Tia as they stood watching Toya make her way down the aisle. "She's beautiful."

"That's my big sis," Tia said with pride.

Gina was holding white Lilies in her hand as Toya came to a full stop in front of the altar. Gina was so happy for her friend. She even smiled at the thought that mother and father were marrying daughter and son, but while all of this was beautiful, it was not for her.

Pastor Yvonne stood in front of her daughter. Toya's fiancé was next to her as she said, "Dearly beloved, we are gathered here in the sight of God, and in the presence of family and friends to join together Jarrod Reed and Toya Milner in Holy Matrimony, which is an honorable estate, instituted by God and therefore is not to be entered into lightly or unadvisedly, but reverently, joyfully and in the love of God. Into this holy estate, these two persons present come now to be joined."

Pastor Yvonne and Pastor Thomas switched places. Now Pastor Thomas was standing next to his son. Gina smiled at the thought of how weird people on the outside might think this whole thing was. Because since Yvonne and Thomas were now married, Toya and Jarrod should consider themselves sister and brother. But what people on the outside looking in didn't know was that Toya and Jarrod had loved each other since they were kids, their parents hadn't fallen for each other until their respective spouses had passed away. So, Toya and Jarrod decided to let their parents be happy and to allow themselves to also be happy and in love.

Pastor Thomas lovingly gazed over at his wife as he asked, "Who gives this woman to be married?"

"I do," Pastor Yvonne said as she placed a kiss on Toya's cheek.

Toya then stepped forward and stood next to Jarrod. He took her hand in his, lifted it to his lips, and kissed it. "I love you," Jarrod mouthed to his betrothed.

Gina didn't know what that gestured did for Toya, but it warmed her heart. Her friends had found love. But then her eyes shifted, and she looked over at David Pittman. He and Jarrod had been college roommates. David had been the big jock on campus that everyone knew would go pro, so women swarmed him. Which was probably the reason he was always in the media dealing with drama from one woman after the other. Gina rolled her eyes at the thought of men like David, who thought they could possess any woman they wanted.

She turned her attention back to the happy occasion as Pastor Thomas opened his Bible and read from 1 Corinthians 13:4-8, "Love is patient, love is kind. It does not envy, it does not boast, it is not proud. It is not rude, it is not self-seeking, it is not easily angered, it keeps no record of wrongs. Love does not delight in evil but rejoices with the truth. It always protects, always trusts, always hopes, always perseveres. Love never fails."

Gina wanted to contradict every word that Pastor Thomas just read. But he'd read from the Bible, and since Gina was a Christian, she believed every word printed in the Bible was inspired by God. So, those words must be true. But she'd never known a love like that. Love had been impatient, rude, angry, and totally self-seeking. No man had ever just loved her for the sake of loving. The Bible told her that 'love never fails'. But it had failed her.

As Toya and Jarrod said, 'I do' and kissed, a tear rolled down Gina's face. Others may have thought she cried because of the sweet moment they all just shared with the love birds. But Gina's tears were because this was one piece of the Bible that she didn't believe a word of.

~~~

David's eyes were wet as Jarrod strutted out of the church with his new wife. It had been a beautiful ceremony. But as David's father used to tell him, 'some men find gold, others get lumps of coal'.

When they finished with everything at the church, David got back in his car and drove to the reception hall. On his way, he put in a call to Katie. "Hey, I'm on my way to the wedding reception, so I don't have long to talk."

Katie was not happy. "This is serious business, David. You're treating this like it can wait, but I assure you it can't."

"I'm not ignoring you. I get it. The contract is in jeopardy, but it's not my fault. I didn't do what I'm being accused of."

"I know you didn't do it. Do you think I'd still be working for you if I thought you were that kind of pig?"

"Good, so go convince the board of directors at the Foodie network that I'm not a pig, and we're all good."

Katie harrumphed. "I wish it was that simple." Then she snapped her finger. "Hold on, wait a minute. I can't tell them, and you can't tell them, but maybe if we could find a way to get some good press, then they will see the real David Pittman."

"How much time do we have to change their minds?"

"The board has set your contract aside until their next meeting. Which won't be until the end of next month."

He pulled up to the reception hall and parked his car. "Okay. Let me finish celebrating my college buddy's wedding and then we can put our heads together on this tomorrow."

In truth, celebrating his college buddy wasn't the only reason David was anxious to get into the reception hall. He noticed this cute honey watching him during the wedding. It didn't feel right to push up on her at the church, but the reception hall didn't have a sanctuary or an altar. His grandmother taught him not to play with God and to always respect God's house.

David took his place with the bridal party as they lined up to greet the new Mr. & Mrs. Jarrod Reed as they made their grand entrance. Everyone applauded for them because they made such a beautiful couple. David was still tripping at how Jarrod had finally gotten the girl of his dreams.

And Toya was a good one. She wasn't a gold digger like so many of the women he dated. She had her stuff together, had started her own law firm, and didn't ask his boy for a dime to make it happen.

He turned his attention to the woman who had been checking him out earlier at the church. At first, he thought she was just a cutie, but David had to correct himself because the woman standing in front of him was fine. That coal-black hair and the angular cut with bangs across her forehead was a real regal look. Her pouty lips with that shimmery lip gloss all the bridesmaids were wearing was so kissable on her.

Instead of going straight for the kiss as he would have done in his college years and definitely during his pro-ball years, he stuck his hand out. "I thought we should meet since we're both in the wedding party. I'm David Pittman."

Dismissing his extended hand, she smirked. "I should have known you were one of the groom's men. But you were too full of yourself to show up for the rehearsal."

"My boy understood that I had responsibilities," David said, then he leaned back and gave her a hard stare. "I'm full of myself, am I? And how would you know that?"

She put a hand on her hip, rolled her eyes heavenward. "Because you kissed me when we were in college… without asking, you just went in for one."

"You say that like it was a bad thing?" David tried to joke, but when he took note of the angry look on her face, he cleared his throat. "I'm sorry. Look, I only did that stuff when I was drinking. That's probably why I don't remember you. You'll be happy to know that I don't drink anymore, nor do I accost unsuspecting women."

"That's not what the tabloids say," she shot back.

"You can't believe everything you read. I'm sorry to have bothered you. Back in college and now," David said and then walked away.

~~~

Gina didn't go around offending people. That's not who she was. But it galled her that the jerk didn't even remember her, after how he had locked lips with her in college. And then to use the excuse of being drunk, like that absolved him of bad behavior. But as the night wore on, she had a tinge of guilt about being so rude.

"Gina, have I got some good news for you," Toya had changed out of her floor-length wedding gown and was now wearing a white knee-length dress with fringe.

"I could use some good news today, what is it?"

"Didn't you tell me you're looking for new clients?"

"Yes, ma'am. I thank the Lord that I know Jesus or else I'd be doing something strange for a piece of change right about now," she joked.

"I didn't know it's been so hard for you lately. Why didn't you tell me?"

Gina waved the thought away. "Girl, please, you've been getting ready for your big day. I wasn't about to ruin that with my problems."

Toya gave her friend a disapproving look. "You know if you need anything, all you have to do is ask."

"Okay, tell me more about this potential client."

3

"And you're sure that your friend knows her stuff?" David couldn't believe his good fortune. He had come to Jarrod's wedding reception when everything in him said to hop on the next thing smoking and get back to Dallas. Katie was right, he needed to get to work repairing his image so he could get this contract signed.

"I've never used her firm. But Gina is A-1 solid. She'll get you done," Jarrod guaranteed. Just then, Toya walked over to them, with Gina following behind. Jarrod then asked, "You remember Gina Melson from college, don't you?"

David reached into his jacket pocket and pulled out his business card. When he glanced back up, his eyes widened as he looked into the beautiful face of a woman who thought he was nothing more than a jerk. She couldn't stand him, and he thought she was one rude lady. He doubted that they could work together. But he didn't want to make things any more awkward than they already were, so he handed her the business card. "Hi Gina, I've heard good things about your public relations company. If you're interested, give me a call."

When she didn't respond, David took the card back and wrote on the back. "Better yet, I'm giving you my business manager's email address. Send her your resume and some samples of your work. She'll get back with you if it's what we're looking for."

"I can do that. Thank you," Gina put the business card in her purse. "I'll let you boys continue talking," she said as she looped her hand around Toya's arm and pulled her with her as they walked away.

He didn't like the way she called them 'boys'. Like they were acting like boys rather than being the grown men they most definitely were.

"She'll send her information. You can count on Gina," Jarrod told him.

"She didn't even ask me what I needed." David tried not to sound annoyed, but Gina had rubbed him the wrong way. He would tell Katie to just ignore any email she received from her. He'd had enough of women like her.

~~~

Why on earth did the potential client have to be David Pittman? She really needed a gig, but could she lower her standards to work with someone like him? But when she arrived home found the eviction notice taped to her front door, she stopped worry about her standards and became more concerned with self-preservation. Gina was thankful that her mother had let her keep the car. Because if she had dropped Gina off, she might have come in the house with her and then seen the eviction notice taped to the front door.

She sat down at her dining room table, opened her laptop, and googled David. She knew that he had been a wide receiver in the NFL and that he was now some type of celebrity chef with guest appearances on local talk shows, cooking shows. David Pittman was making it do what it do. He even had a restaurant in Ann Arbor, Michigan, and Dallas, Texas. Gina thought that was an ego thing because David picked the towns he had played college ball and professional ball to open restaurants.

He was beloved in Michigan because he was on the 2003 team that beat Ohio State. He could do no wrong as far as the people in these parts felt. He was the hometown boy who made good. Gina copied and pasted a picture of the restaurant, which was called End Zone in her proposal. She added a few statements about how much David was loved in Michigan and Texas, but as a plug for herself, she made sure to state ways in which she thought his brand could be taken nationwide. With the right PR, David could open End Zones in five more states and feel confident that the public would pay to eat at his restaurants.

Gina was desperate and didn't have time to play around and pretend that she had so much work that it would take her a week or two to put a proposal together. She stayed up all night working on it. By five in the morning, her eyes were drooping and red. But she still managed to hit send on the proposal that went to David's business manager. Now she would wait to hear from her so she could further state her case for why she was the perfect person for the job.

As she stood up, Gina glanced over at the eviction notice. She would have to come up with the rent or go to court on the 15th of January. She wasn't going to let her current situation get her in a funk. Gina had prayed and asked God to help her, she just had to trust that the God she served was not only willing but more than able to do even more than what she could think or ask.

She laid down to get a few hours of sleep before church service at 10 a.m. that morning. No matter how bad things got, or how bad she was feeling, entering the house of the Lord always made things seem a little brighter. She wasn't trying to miss service, so she set her alarm for eight-thirty.

Her phone rang at eight-twenty. Yawning and stretching, Gina reached for it. If Katie was responding to her proposal, she didn't want to miss the call. "This is Gina Melson," she answered without looking at the caller ID.

"You sound sleepy. I thought you'd be up getting ready for church by now."

It was her mother. "I stayed up late working on a proposal for a potential client."

"Potential client, huh. So, do you think you might get this assignment?" her mom asked.

Gina knew her mom was worried because of the car issue, so she wanted to ease her concerns. "It looks good. I got the lead at the wedding last night. Networking normally pays off."

"I sure hope so, because your father and I are worried about you."

"Stop worrying. I should only need to keep the car for about a week or so, and I'll have my car back, I promise," Gina hoped her words were reassuring, then she asked, "How is dad doing? It seemed like he was using his inhaler a lot when I was at the house last week."

"He was. The doctor put him back on oxygen. That's partly why I'm calling this morning. Your dad and I talked last night, we're going to put the house up for sale."

Gina popped up in the bed as she tried to open her bloodshot eyes. "But you love that house. You said it was the last house you ever wanted to live in."

"I know," her mom agreed with a sad undertone in her voice. "But things change."

"What could have possibly changed to make you want to move out of your dream home, Mom?" Audrey and George Melson had lived in that three-bedroom brick house since Gina was in elementary. Her mom had remodeled several times and always seemed to love it more after each remodel.

Sighing, Audrey confided in her daughter, "Your dad needs another surgery. We just can't afford all the co-pays without selling the house."

Gina felt awful. All she'd ever wanted to do was make enough money to be able to care for her parents. They had sacrificed so much to send her to college. Gina knew that her parents didn't make much money, so when the full scholarship didn't materialize, she thought she would have to give up her dream of going to college. But her parents told her that the only dream she had to give up was going to an out-of-state college.

Out-of-state colleges were three times more expensive as in-state colleges. So, Gina went to the University of Michigan. Her partial scholarship paid for everything except her room and board and books. Her parents worked two and three jobs to make up the difference. "Don't put the house up for sale just yet. I might be getting a new client, depending on the extent of the job, I should be able to cover the bill for you."

"You have your own bills. If you want to know the truth about it, we wish we had the money to give you so you could get your car back. But with all the medical bills, we just don't have it. We can't help with that and we sure aren't about to stick you with our bills on top of your own."

"You're not sticking me with anything. If I have to give up my apartment and move back home so I can pay his hospital bill, then I'll do that." And since she already had an eviction notice, Gina might be moving home sooner rather than later anyway.

She hung up the phone with her mother, got out of bed, and dressed for church. Toya and Jarrod would be touching down in

Belize by the time she got to church because they took a flight out at five this morning.

Gina had to hurry. She was thankful that her mother's Toyota Camry was outside waiting on her. It was a long way from her BMW, but it would get her where she needed to go, so Gina wasn't tripping, getting to church was all that mattered. She was going straight to the altar and telling God all about her troubles. If He wasn't hearing her prayers from home, He would certainly listen to them at the altar. At least, Gina hoped He would.

~~~

"Okay, let's get to it. What do we have?" David asked as he sat in the conference room with Katie.

Katie spread several manilla folders out on the table. "I've narrowed it down to three PR firms that we might be able to use. She handed him one of the folders. "The Peterson Touch Firm has a good reputation, so I think they could get the job done."

David narrowed his gaze on Katie. "You don't seem impressed. So, if they are such a good firm, what's wrong with them."

"Their presentation was lackluster at best. Like they didn't have time to pull together a complete proposal for us. Most of the information they provided was generic. I just don't see you being their main focus, and we don't have time to sit around waiting on them.

"Right, the board meets again next month." David placed the Peterson Touch folder back on the table. "Who else you got?"

Handing him another folder, Katie said, "Fame is another firm that has gotten results for their clients. They deal with high profile clients who are always getting themselves into some kind of drama. So, my concern is that you wouldn't be a top priority for them either."

Looking through the proposal, David said, "But they have a hundred people on staff. You don't think that's enough?"

"They may have a hundred on staff, but they only have twenty PR executives. The rest work on admin duties, accounting, and marketing stuff." Katie shrugged. "They may be the perfect firm for our needs. My concern is that with all the employees they have on staff, how many of them would be able to get hold of your information and then leak it to the press or blackmail you at a later date. I'm just leery of that many people with our personal PR needs."

"Yeah, you might be right about that." David leaned back in his chair. "You said you were interested in three. Who's next?"

"Truthfully, I am interested in one more. But we'll talk about that in a minute." She opened the third folder and put it on the table in front of him. "This is a small boutique. I like that about them. They've been in business for five years, so they have a track record, and I like that."

"Okay, so that's the good news."

"How do you know there's bad news." Katie shoved his chair. "I'm not some negative Nancy, you know."

"I know that. But I also know how you roll. You like to prime the pump with the good news, then dash my hopes with the bad." He lifted his hands and made that come-on-with-it motion with his fingers.

"It's not my fault that we don't need the kind of help this firm is offering," Katie shot back.

"What does that mean, Katie, my lady."

She smiled at the term of endearment. "Flattery won't get you very far today. Because this firm submitted a proposal that brands you as a football superstar."

It was now David's turn to shrug. "What's wrong with that?"

"Nothing, if you're auditioning for another wide receiver position or if you want to become an analyst on ESPN. But the PR campaign we need is one that will get the folks at the Foodie network to sit up and take notice."

David was getting frustrated; he clasped his hands together. "Why are we even discussing these firms if you don't like any of them?"

"Because you won't let me accept the firm that I really like, so we're left with all of these good for some, but bad for you options."

"Are you back on Gina Melson again?"

Katie picked up the last folder she brought into the conference room and handed it to David. "Her firm is called, It's About YOU. And the 'you' is in all caps for a reason, David. This woman has a small boutique, but she works with her clients based on their needs, not her own perceived formula for success."

"She's rude."

Katie took the folder out of David's hand and placed it on the table in front of him. She opened it. "Just look at some of the campaigns she's done for her clients. Look at the testimonials. Even the proposal that she put together for your PR campaign shows that she gets you. She recognizes that you were once a superstar football hero with fans in Michigan and Texas, but she also understands that we need to expand our PR campaign and do things that will have a more national appeal."

David pushed his chair back and stood. "I don't care. Give the campaign to one of the other firms and just tell them to do the things Gina proposed."

Appalled at his suggestion, she said, "I'm not going to give It's About YOU's ideas to another firm. Do you know how fast you'd be hit with a lawsuit?"

David shook his head. Gina was too judgmental. And she was probably still mad that he didn't remember some kiss. Nope, she was not the person for this job. "Then let that other firm dress me up like a football and have kids toss me around in their back yard. I'm out. Just pick one and let's do something about our little problem."

As David opened the door and walked out of the room, Katie yelled back at him, "It's not just a 'little problem'. This is a big deal that could sink your next big move. This is our last chance to get this right."

4

Gina had prayed, she shouted, she praised God and cried out to Him all while wondering why nothing was breaking for her. She just didn't understand why there was no response from the proposals she'd sent out. Because she hadn't just sent the one to David, but within the last week she'd sent out five different proposals. It did bother her that she hadn't received a response from David or his business manager, because Gina thought for sure that David would put in a word for her since they went to the same college. But she couldn't even get his business manager to return her calls.

As she sat in her home office on New Year's Eve staring at her computer, waiting for an email to pop up, she suddenly had a thought. What if she was in the wrong career? Or if this move back to Michigan was all wrong for her. Don't they always say in church that if God gives the vision, He'll provide the provision? So, maybe as the year 2020 rolls in, she needed to reflect on a new career that could pay the bills.

Gina had always been the type of person to want to fix a problem when she encountered one. This is why public relations had been a good fit for her for so many years. She could analyze her client's problems and then come up with solutions that fit the need. She wished she could use that same skill to help herself. Because Gina wasn't sure at this moment if it was the career or if it was the city that had caused her decline in revenue. She needed to figure something out soon, or she just might be filling out an application to scan groceries at Walmart.

The bell chimed on her computer, letting her know that she had a message in the inbox. Swiveling around in her chair, Gina quickly glanced at the computer screen, praying that one of the people she sent a proposal to was finally responding. But that was not the case. It was a Happening In Your Hood e-newsletter. Gina read this newsletter each month when she received it because it provided good leads for potential clients. However, they had sent out their monthly newsletter last week, so she was surprised to see another one so soon.

Gina opened the newsletter more out of ritual than any great expectation. Her hopes had been dashed so many times in the past that she almost feared hoping for the best. When Gina was in college, she volunteered as a mentor for underprivileged children. A girl she mentored told her that she feared getting her hopes up, only to have everything fall apart again. Gina hadn't understood how anyone could so thoroughly lose hope like that. But that was when everything was coming up like roses for her.

Happening In Your Hood didn't have any articles in this newsletter; actually, it wasn't even a newsletter today, more like an advertisement or a flyer. But the flyer did surprise her. David Pittman was doing a New Year's Eve event at his restaurant in Ann Arbor. However, his event wasn't taking place tonight, but beginning at noon and ending at four pm. Ann Arbor was a little under an hour away. If she got dressed now, she might be able to get there and talk to him in person. "Please, God, let this flyer mean that something good is about to happen." Was she allowing herself to hope again?

Gina shook her head. She had no time to think about the inconsistencies of her brain. She had to get dressed and get herself to that restaurant. But before leaving out of the house, Gina sent the flyer about David's event along with his bio to her old boss from her first PR job. Lisa Harris was no longer a public relations executive at their old firm. She was now a producer on a hit chef competition show that had gone nationwide. She prayed that Lisa was in the office this morning and that somehow, someway, she would be able to help her.

When Gina arrived at the End Zone, she was amused at the sight of David dressed as a football player, throwing the football to customers like he was on a football field. On the other side of the room, some guy was snapping pictures with his cell phone and giving play calls. The people in the restaurant were trying to eat their lunch while this spectacle was going on.

Then the man yelled out from behind his cell phone/camera, "Tell us about the big game."

No die-hard Michigan fan ever had to be told about 'The Game'. Ohio State was Michigan's biggest rival; whenever they played, excitement was in the air. Ohio State had just stomped Michigan at the end of November, and many fans were still licking their wounds from that game. But in 2003, Michigan beat Ohio State with a score of thirty-five to twenty-one. And David ran almost a hundred yards in that game, so he was a big factor in the win.

Shaking his head, David said, "Carl, these people don't want to hear about a game that happened sixteen years ago."

A man seated in the front of the restaurant stood up and yelled out, "After the game we just watched last month, we need something to cheer us up."

People started pounding on the tables and chanting. "Tell the story… tell the story."

The hostess made her way back to the waiting area. She apologized for the delay, but Gina hadn't noticed how long she'd been standing, because she'd been too busy watching the show. The hostess sat Gina at a table close to the kitchen. She looked at the menu and saw things like Big Mama's Shrimp and Grits, Bird Dog's Famous Cheesesteak, Jarrod's Crabby Cakes. As she looked further down the menu, she noticed that Big Mama also had a sweet potato cheesecake. For some reason, David had named his menu items after people he knew personally.

There was also a Joe's Akin Bacon, which was a BLT sandwich named after one of his teammates at Michigan. She ordered the BLT and then turned her attention back to David as he entertained his audience by recounting his former glory at the University of Michigan. As she watched, Gina had to admit, the man was quite charming. He certainly could work a room, that gorgeous smile of his didn't hurt either.

He finished his story and was about to move away from the crowd when Carl approached him again. Gina saw the irritation in David's face as he was instructed to do something that he obviously didn't agree with. But Gina didn't understand how he could have agreed with anything he had been asked to do since she arrived. He was a true spectacle, Gina wasn't sure David wasn't getting the effect that he wanted when beginning his PR campaign.

Storming away from Carl, David headed toward the kitchen. He passed her, but then his head jerked back as he turned and walked back to her table. "Spying on me?"

"Now, why would I ever want to watch you re-live your glory days, acting like you're on a football field rather than in a restaurant?"

The waitress brought Gina's sandwich to the table as David sat down across from her. If she wasn't here to beg for a job, she would ask why he thought he could just sit at her table without asking if that seat was available. But she had already scoffed at this whole football event he was having in his restaurant, so she wasn't going to push her luck.

"Why are you so rude to me, Gina? What have I done that was so bad?"

"Well, at least you remembered my name today," she laughed. Then she took a bite of her sandwich. "Oh my God, this is good." She talked while chewing her sandwich.

"I'm glad you like it." He smiled at her enjoyment.

She took another bite and then licked some of the sauce off her lips. "What's in this sauce?"

"It's a little heat and a little sweet."

"I'd eat this every day of the week. But why'd you name it after Joe?"

"Did you know Joe?" David asked.

"We just spoke in passing. I tried not to hang around too many jocks on campus."

Nodding, as if he understood, David said, "If you'd hung around my old college buddy, you'd know that he absolutely loved bacon. So, in memory of my friend, I added a BLT to the menu."

"You didn't just add a BLT to the menu. You perfected it. I know someone who loves bacon too." She took a picture of what was left of her sandwich and then used her phone to text something about the sandwich.

"I'm glad I managed to do something you approve of. On your way out, you might want to check out my wall of trust. Those people actually think well of me, as I do of them." He waved an arm around the room where framed pictures hung on the wall, in different sizes from eight by tens to life-size photos. He then pushed his chair back, getting ready to stand.

Wiping her hands with the napkin, Gina realized why she wasn't getting a response to her proposal. David didn't like her. Like it was her fault that he was so obnoxious in college. "Look, I get it. We got off on the wrong foot the other day. But we will be celebrating a new year tomorrow, so can't we just forgive and forget. Hey, at least I didn't make you put on a football jersey and run around here like one of those pathetic guys who can't get over themselves and has to relive his glory days to make himself feel better about his life."

David put his elbow on the table with chin in hand. "That swift tongue of yours moves quickly from flattery to insult, doesn't it?"

She lifted a hand. "I'm not trying to insult you. I just don't understand why you didn't at least look at my proposal, because I wouldn't have done this to you." She pointed at his uniform. "To build your brand, you need to leverage the fact that you were *once,*" she emphasized the word 'once' "a superstar football player in order to open doors that can get you national attention. But you don't want to try to reenact your glory days. That's taking you backward. Because Michigan and Texas already love you."

"And I suppose you can do better."

Her phone dinged, Gina picked the phone up and smiled as she read the text. "Of course, I can do better. I already have and you haven't even hired me yet."

"Yet?"

Gina handed him her phone and let him read the text. "The person I know who loves bacon has a spot available for you on The Grind." The Grind was a show like Chopped. Accept the cooking contest wasn't the only factor in picking the winner. The first show was all about cooking. But the winner of that show was given a ticket to compete in the grand finale. This grand finale provided free marketing to restaurant owners and executive chefs because the grand finale highlighted the chef's restaurant, hence the name. The Grind was meant to represent the work that chefs put in to make a success out of their big idea. The Grind also let the chef highlight the charity they would give half of their fifty thousand dollar winnings too.

Sputtering, David asked, "H-how did you get them to agree to this? I tried to get on The Grind last year so I could highlight the restaurant I had just opened in Dallas, but it never worked out."

Gina could hardly believe that she pulled this off. If she hadn't known someone on that show and hadn't ordered that BLT, she might not have received a response to her query. But she wasn't about to say that to him. "Give me a chance, David. Let me show you what I can do to get you the national attention you deserve."

"What if I lose on The Grind? Won't that be bad for my brand?"

"It's a chance you have to take. You've been competing all your life. Don't tell me you're suddenly afraid of a little competition?"

"Mr. Pittman, we're ready for pictures in the photo booth area," Carl told him.

David looked as if he wanted to fire the man right then and there. But instead, he told him, "I'll be right there." He then waved a waitress over to their table. When the waitress arrived, he said, "Give Ms. Melson another BLT to go and anything else she wants, it's on me."

"I'll take that sandwich, thank you very much." She pulled her business card out of her purse. "And when you're ready to do a national campaign, give me a call. But I'm not sure how long The Grind will wait for an answer."

Nodding, his eyes brightened with admiration. "I see you've got skills."

Before he walked away, Gina asked, "What charity would you like to bring awareness to on the show? It should be something that could also mix in with…"

"Alzheimer," he said before Gina could finish her pitch for the perfect charity.

"Allll-right, Alzheimer's, it is." She jotted that info in the notes tab on her phone. Thanked the waitress as she handed her the BLT. But before leaving the restaurant, she did as David suggested. She checked out his wall of trust.

Gina was sure it was just a braggadocios wall, that would show him taking pictures with high profile celebrities so that he could let all of the little people know how much of a celebrity he, himself was. But as she approached the wall, she was pleasantly surprised to see that the photos were of friends and family. The same friends and family he had named sandwiches and entrees after. And there was not one picture of David on the wall. It was as if he truly wanted to celebrate the people in his life who must have made some type of impression on him.

As she drove home, Gina wondered if she could fill a wall full of people she liked and who liked her. She had kept to herself for so long after escaping the abuse of a man she definitely didn't like or trust. She could put her mom and dad on that wall... Toya and Jarrod. But after that, she'd have to think a while to come up with anyone else. Life just hadn't been as kind to her as it had been to David.

But then she thought about Jesus and smiled. David may have his wall and a bunch of friends and family who loved him, but she had Jesus and that was good enough for her.

5

"No! No! Get away from me!" Gina tossed and turned as she fought off her attacker. "You can't do this to me. I don't belong to you anymore. I belong to God."

Gina's eyes flashed open as she jolted upright in bed. Panting and gasping for breath, she made note of her surroundings. She wasn't being kicked and choked by Marvel. She was in her own bed having a nightmare. "When will it end, Lord. When will the memory of that man be wiped away? I don't want to remember the pain of those days and all the bad decisions I made back then."

It was just six in the morning, but Gina got out of bed and drove to the gym. She needed to do something to cleanse her mind. When she was on the treadmill walking, then jogging, then taking on a full runner's pace her mind went blank. She didn't think about her bills, her bad decisions, her abusive ex, nothing but the run.

When she arrived back home, she made herself a cup of Macha green tea, and then went into her study, picked up her Bible and sat in her comfy chair. She propped her feet up on the ottoman in front of her chair and began reading from Ephesians chapter 1. Gina loved reading this chapter because it reminded her that no matter how bad she tried to screw up her life, God still chose her, He redeemed her and forgave her. Getting cozy and sipping her tea, Gina began reading at verse three.

Praise be to the God and Father of our Lord Jesus Christ, who has blessed us in the heavenly realms with every spiritual blessing in Christ. For He chose us in Him before the creation of the world to be holy and blameless in His sight. In love He predestined us for adoption to sonship through Jesus Christ, in accordance with his pleasure and will— to the praise of his glorious grace, which He has freely given us in the One He loves. In Him we have redemption through His blood, the forgiveness of sins, in accordance with the riches of God's grace that He lavished on us.

Gina hadn't lived a blameless life. She had dated the guy she knew her best friend was in love with. And when that didn't pan out the way she'd hoped, she bounced around from one guy to the next. In truth, she hadn't been mad at David for kissing her back then, she allowed it because she wanted to brag about how she and David were dating. But just as he didn't recognize her at the wedding, he hadn't remembered the incident when she saw him on campus the next day.

In truth, David was the reason Gina shied away from jocks during college. She realized pretty quickly that jocks like David didn't care about anyone but themselves. But that didn't stop her from partying. Gina did a lot of that in college. And then she really turned away from everything she'd been taught growing up in church once she left college and met Marvel. But God showed her grace anyway. The knowledge of that brought tears to her eyes.

She hugged the Bible to her chest. "Thank You, Jesus. Things aren't all of what I want them to be right now. But at least I have

You." Gina took a napkin off the table, wiped the tears from her face, then blew her nose. The Word was sweet, and it revived her spirit.

As she put the Bible down Gina, was reminded of something. She had woke up to a brand-new year. It was now 2020 and she had a chance for a do-over, or at least that's how the beginning of each year always felt to her. She went into her office and took one of her unused journals off the shelf and then went back to her study, sat in her comfy chair and began to write out some of the great expectations she had for the new year. She wasn't writing resolutions because people broke those within a few weeks of writing them down.

Gina's first great expectation was to have a business that was flourishing. She wrote, "I am an asset to my clients, and they gladly refer other businesses to me. Enough money flows into my business so that I can pay my tithes, for my household needs, car and all other bills, and then have plenty left over to sow seeds into people and ministries."

The next great expectation was a little trickier. She didn't know how God would work it out, given her track record with men. But after witnessing Toya and Jarrod's wedding and seeing how in love they were, she didn't want to miss out on something that could be wonderful, so she wrote down her next great expectation, "I am married to a man who loves me like Christ loves the church. My man would lay down his life to protect me. My man would never do anything to harm or hurt me." Taking a deep breath, Gina nodded in affirmation, yes, that was what she wanted. And she believed that with God on her side, she could not only have a successful career but a loving marriage.

She was just getting ready to write down her next great expectation when the phone rang. She didn't recognize the number, but giving the journal she was working on, she had great expectations as she answered the phone. "This is Gina Melson, can I help you?"

"Good morning Ms. Melson. This is Katie Perkins. I am David Pittman's business manager."

A smile crept across Gina's face. Yes, thank You, Lord. Keep doing what You do, she said silently to her savior, then to Katie, as calmly as she could, she said, "How can I help you?"

"Mr. Pittman informed me that you were able to get him an invite on The Grind. Is this correct?"

"Yes, it is. But if he's going to do the show, they need an answer by today. And he will need to be there in two days."

"Why so soon?"

"They had a cancellation, so they were just about to fill the spot when I contacted them."

"I just don't understand how you were able to get him on that show so quickly. I have been sending information to those people for the past year trying to get David a spot, but nothing moved for him."

Gina was about to be coy and pretend that she was just that good and would even be able to deliver bigger shows if they signed with her. But she couldn't bring herself to fake it. "Sometimes it's just the luck of the draw. But in this case, I use to work for one of the producers of that show. So, I pitched an angel to her and she loved it. Now, I can't promise that lightning will strike twice and that I'll be able to get any other national shows to take notice, but if you give me a chance, I will do my best with Mr. Pittman's PR campaign. I certainly can do a better job than what I witnessed yesterday."

Katie started laughing, "Yesterday was awful. I'm glad I wasn't there, the clips I saw on his Facebook page were enough for me."

"Why on earth did he decide to use a firm that would focus on his previous career to get him publicity?"

"It was a mistake, but I like your honesty, Gina. We'd very much like to work with you. Can you fax your contract and your retainer requirements?"

Pumping her fist in the air, Gina was thrilled. Katie had said the magic word, 'retainer'. "I will get it to you today. Would you like me to accept The Grind's offer, or would you like to do that yourself?"

"If you can send the information to me, I would very much like to make contact, then I will send the itinerary, flight and hotel information to you and David."

Gina didn't expect this. She didn't want to be out of town for any long period of time. Not with her father needing an operation soon. "I didn't know you'd want me to travel with Mr. Pittman."

"I just need you there for a day. You and I need to discuss the focus of David's campaign. He needs more than just national appearances, and I think you're the person to handle our needs."

"Great. I will see you tomorrow. Let me get my contract over to you." They hung up and Gina danced around the house.

~~~

A happy client was a paying client was what her former boss and mentor once told her. And today, Gina made it her business to thank Lisa for helping her to get another paying gig. But Lisa wasn't having it.

"Don't you thank me. You sent over a good package with a really good angel. But what I want to know is, how did you know we had a cancellation for the bacon competition?"

Gina shook her head. "I didn't. But when I bit into that sandwich, and I remembered how much you used to love BLTs, I gave it a shot and text you the picture."

"I thought you had actually done your research. But God must have been on your side with that one."

"Well, at least accept my thank you gift." Gina handed Lisa the BLT that she had David make specially for her this morning before they flew to New York to tape the show.

Lisa's eyes bugged out. "Is that the sandwich you sent me a picture of?"

"You know it. I had David make it for you this morning."

Lisa took the sandwich from Gina and then held onto it like she would protect it with her life if need be. "I've got to take care of a few things before the show starts, and I'm going to see if this sandwich is as good as you say."

"Okay." Giggling at her former boss, Gina added. "One of these days, you'll learn to take my word." When Gina worked for Lisa, the one thing that drove her crazy was that the woman never accepted any of the information Gina brought her unless it had been verified by at least three other sources. But Lisa's over-demanding habits had helped her when it came to researching her client's needs.

As she watched Lisa walk away, something struck her that she hadn't paid much attention to when Lisa said it, but now it made sense. Her former boss told her that God must have been on her side since she was at the right place, ordering the right sandwich at the right time. For weeks now, Gina had been wondering if God was listening to her prayers. She didn't need a lightning bolt to strike to prove to her that God was in the prayer answering business. She was supposed to run into David at the wedding because they were meant to help each other. She said it often, but didn't mind saying it again, "Thank You, Jesus."

"What was that?"

Gina turned around to greet a white woman with auburn hair and the prettiest green eyes she'd ever seen standing in front of her waiting on an answer to the question she'd just posed. "Oh, I was just being thankful." Gina put a hand out to the woman. "I'm Gina Melson, can I help you with something?"

"Hi Gina, I'm Katie."

"Oh, wow! Hi Katie." Gina hugged the woman. "Thanks for taking care of the travel arrangements."

"Not a problem." Katie looked back toward the area where David and the other two contestants were standing. "He'll be busy here for a while, but I have procured a conference room where you and I can talk. Is that okay?"

Gina really wanted to stay and watch David cook his heart out. She prayed he would win, but Katie was holding a folder that Gina thought might contain her check, so she wasn't about to delay this meeting. "Yes, I'm fine with that."

They took the elevator to the third floor and went into the conference room that was two doors down from the elevator. They sat down and Katie put the folder on the table. "I printed out the contract, and David has already signed off on your retainer check."

Gina wanted to leap for joy. She always requested a five thousand dollar retainer. This would pay the two months she was behind on rent, the three months on the car, and if she could keep this gig for six months, she would for sure be able to take care of her father's hospital bills. "Thank you for taking care of this. Now I can get to work on truly building David's brand."

Katie lifted a hand, slowing Gina's roll. "I noticed that your contract is for six months. But you need to understand that these next twenty-eight days are most important to us."

Gina's hopes were dashing right before her eyes. "So, you only need my services for a month? There's no way I could get him the kind of PR that would build a national brand in just a month. Are you being serious… or is this just because David and I got off on the wrong foot?"

Katie opened the folder, handed Gina the check, then flipped through a few pages on the contract.

Gina used the moment as her opportunity to plead her case. "I know David only gave me the job because I was able to get him on The Grind, but I can do so much more."

"I don't doubt it, Gina. And believe me, I'm in your corner. It's just that the decision as to whether or not David will get his own show on the Foodie Network will be determined at the board meeting at the end of this month. That's why we really need to get his name out there in a hurry.

"Now, if he gets his show approved, then we will need your help for several months to comes. Can you work with us on that basis?"

Gina didn't want to come off as greedy or ungrateful for this opportunity, but she had to make sure she could cover things for herself and her parents until she could get another assignment so she said, "I appreciate this opportunity, but if I am going to build the type of campaign you need for this month, I will not be able to take on any other clients so I will have to insist on having a guarantee of at least three months. Can you work with that?" Gina silently prayed that they could work with that because she was all out of answers.

Please work with it, please work with it, was the chant going on in Gina's head as Katie wrote something on the contract, signed it, then passed it to her. Katie had scratched out the six-month guarantee and scribbled in a three-month guarantee with a possibility to renew the next three months. "Thank you," Gina said as the realization that she finally had another paying client sunk in.

"Don't thank me yet, I haven't told you why we need your help." Before I can discuss anything further, I need you to sign this non-disclosure agreement."

6

At first, Gina thought she was being asked to not disclose the fact that she was doing public relations for David Pittman. That would be out of the question because she planned to get her next gig by billing herself as the PR firm that built David Pittman's new brand. "Are you saying I can't promote the fact that I am working with David. That would be very disappointing because this is just a short-term contract. But having this contract will help my firm, secure other clients."

Shaking her head, Katie told her, "We don't want to stop you from growing your business; that's not what this non-disclosure is about. David is dealing with some sensitive issues. I need to tell you about those issues so you understand our needs while putting together a public relations campaign that will get results."

"Okay, I'm listening," was all Gina said, but in truth, she was a bit perplexed because she thought they needed a national campaign. Being a part of The Grind would give them that.

"This information has not been released to the public yet; however, we did have to disclose it to the Foodie Network so we wouldn't be in breach of contract." Katie hesitated for a moment. Took a deep breath. "David is being blackmailed."

Gina was shocked, but she didn't know why she was so shocked. The man she knew of in college lived in a manner worthy of blackmail.

Katie continued, "A woman alleges that she was pregnant by David."

Gina rolled her eyes, "Is that all. In this day we live in it happens all the time."

"Not with David."

Gina wondered how Katie could be so emphatic about something like this. Men slip up all the time. Why was she so sure David had not impregnated this woman?

"But the pregnancy is not our problem. The woman also claims that David became so angry when she refused to have an abortion that he beat her. She has paperwork that proves she was in the hospital and that she lost the baby."

No God, No. I didn't just sign on to work with a monster just like Marvel. You wouldn't allow something like that to happen, would You, Lord? If this was true, no amount of money would be enough for her to stay on this assignment. She put the five thousand dollar check in her purse because she was not giving that back. She did after all get him on The Grind.

Gina signed the non-disclosure and slid it over to Katie. "I will not repeat a word of what you told me, but if this is true, I can't in good conscious work for a monster like him."

"It's not true," Katie assured her. "The woman never mentioned David's name when the police arrived at the hospital to take her statement. It wasn't until three weeks after the hospital incident that she even contacted David with this scheme. So, we believe that whoever her abuser is, he is the one who convinced her to make these claims. They want money, and David is refusing to give it to them."

"And this woman knew about the network deal? Is that why she decided to blackmail rather than go to the police?" Gina was trying to wrap her head around this, was David a monster or a victim of some scheming woman.

"As far as we know, she had no idea about it, but we still had to disclose it to the network. Because if something like that got out after his show was already airing, it would be the end of his career, period."

No doubt. David would truly look like a heartless beast. The same kind of heartless beast that she knew Marvel to be. So, she didn't understand why he didn't just pay the money and move on with his life... unless he really didn't do it. "I need to speak with David before I can commit to going any further. Can you understand that?"

"Completely." Katie stood. "Let's go see if he has managed to get himself a spot on the show."

~~~

David had beat out one opponent and was now going for the win against his last opponent of the day. But the look on Gina's face told him that Katie had spilled the beans. She looked as if she had already put him on trial and found him guilty. If that's the way she felt, David didn't want or need her on his team.

He turned away from Gina's disapproving glare and concentrated on the bacon-flavored ice cream he was creating. His opponent hadn't made many mistakes with her other meal and now she was making a bread pudding with bacon. So, he needed to get his special chocolate muffin and bacon ice cream right if he was going to get in the grand finale.

David took his muffins out of the oven and popped them out of the pan. It was soft and springy. He just hoped it was ooey-gooey goodness when the judges bit into it. David ran over to the ice cream machine, extracted his ice cream, then ran back to his station. Two minutes left. He put the ice cream on his plate and then noticed the bag of cherries still sitting on his station, daring him not to put them on the plate.

"Oh my God, I almost forgot." Hitting his forehead with the palm of his hand, he grabbed a pan, put it on the stove, turned on the fire, then threw the cherries into the pan with some sugar, cinnamon, and a few other spices. Whisking the cherries around and mashing them into a sauce as the clocked ticked down. Sweat dripped from his head as he noted that he only had twenty more seconds. He wanted to blend the cherries to make sure it was smooth enough, but there was no time.

He mashed the cherries one more time and then said a silent prayer as he drizzled the sauce over his muffin. The sauce inadvertently swam around the ice cream as well. The judges would either love it or hate it. Either way, he had no one to blame for leaving those cherries on his station but himself. He'd allowed Gina's disapproving glare to knock him off his game.

The bell rang and they stepped away from the prep tables. David and his opponent stood before the judges. Their food was brought over to the judging tables. He held his breath and waited for his fate.

~~~

"You did it! You did it! I knew you'd win," Katie was jumping around, high-fiving everyone in sight.

David turned to Gina, "What about you? Did you think I was going to win?"

Caught off guard by his pointed question, especially since her mind was on something totally different, Gina turned to see if he was talking to someone else.

"I'm talking to you, Gina."

"I'm sorry, I was confused because I'm the one who sent your information into the show. Why would I do that if I didn't think you could win?"

"Who knows, maybe you wanted to see me fall on my face."

David looked angry and Gina didn't understand why. The man had just won a spot to the grand finale on The Grind. The show would be seen by millions and he would be able to showcase his business and his charity. "Am I missing something? If winning puts you in this kind of mood, then I'd hate to know how you'd be acting if your opponent's bread pudding had cooked all the way through." She was a bit more flippantly than she needed to be, but what did she care. She had her retainer and she wasn't all that sure that she wanted to continue working with David anyway. So if he fired her, well then, he just fired her. And then she could get back to Detroit and see about her father sooner than she expected.

"So you did think I was going to lose?" David demanded.

What was this dude's problem? "I'm not saying that. I didn't even see the whole show because Katie and I were busy for a while. I just heard the judges saying that the two of you were neck and neck until she undercooked her bread pudding." Her hands were now on her hips because she was getting ticked. "Is something else going on that I don't know about?"

"You tell me. You're the one that looked all sour mouthed when you entered the studio. Did you hear something you didn't like during your meeting with Katie?"

As he towered over her looking like every bit of the six-foot-five wide receiver he had been, Gina felt like she was the Biblical David and he was Goliath. Just like David in the Bible, she wasn't afraid of the beast that stood in front of her with nostrils flaring. He would be tamed, or she would knock him upside the head with so many stones he'd think one of them linebackers had hit him. One thing was for sure, she was done letting any man intimidate her. Puffing out her chest and putting both hands on her hips, she was getting ready to let him have it.

Katie jumped in between them. "What has gotten into the two of you? We are still at this studio… in public." She motioned her hands, indicating the area they were standing in and the cameramen that were still hanging around. "This is not helpful."

Gina and David's heads swiveled as they took in their surroundings. Since Gina billed herself as a public relations expert, making her client look bad in public was a hard no. It just wasn't done. Why she kept bantering with this man, she just didn't know. Gina took her hands off her hips and backed down. "I'm sorry, I didn't realize I was looking at you that way."

Whispering his response, David told her, "You were, and it nearly cost me the win. Because I was so focused on the way you were glaring at me that I almost forgot about one of the main ingredients."

Gina hadn't realized that her actions could have such an effect on David. The thought that she could have cost him the win on this show was unacceptable. She put a hand on his arm. "I really am sorry, David. I didn't realize that I was staring at you in an off-putting manner. I promise it will not happen again."

David's shoulders relaxed as he appeared to calm down. "I appreciate that."

Katie clasped her hands together. "Now that that's settled, let's get you to the airport."

David kept his eyes on Gina. "Is it settled?"

"I admit that I have questions for you. But I need to get back to Detroit because my father is scheduled to go into surgery tomorrow. So, can we schedule a meeting in a few days?"

A look of concern crossed David's face. "Is he okay? Is there anything you need from us?"

"Thank you for asking. He's been sick for a while now. It's just something we are dealing with. I'll know more once I get back home."

"Okay, I'll have Katie set an appointment for us later next week."

With that, Gina headed home, hoping that once she and David had their conversation that she would be able to stomach working for him so she could help her parents keep their home.

7

"How was your trip, "Audrey asked as Gina took off her coat and sat down in the living room.

"I got paid, so that's a good thing, right?"

"Are you going to be able to get your car back?"

"Picking it up tomorrow."

Sitting down next to her daughter, Audrey pulled Gina into an embrace. "I wish we could do more to help."

"I know that mom. And I appreciate everything you and dad have done for me. That's why I want to help. And that's why I wanted to talk to you before I check on Dad because you know how he is. He won't take money from me if I try to give it to him directly."

"But we don't need your money, hon. This house is paid off, if we can sell it, we will be able to pay the twenty percent that Medicare requires us to pay."

"Mom, let's talk seriously for a moment. I know dad has pulmonary issues, but has it gotten so bad that he really needs surgery?"

Audrey nodded. "You've seen him. He can barely get around without that oxygen tank. He's gotten weaker. If we let it go on any longer, he may be too weak to get the operation. And the doctors think this lung volume reduction surgery will give him some mobility back and help him breathe on his own."

She didn't like hearing that her father was getting weaker. If she knew anything about these sorts of things, Gina knew that surgery could bring on a heart attack for someone who was too weak to endure it. If her father was going to have this surgery, then it needed to happen fast. "How much does a surgery like this cost?"

"It's almost two hundred thousand. But we've been able to receive about sixty thousand in aid. So after Medicare pays their portion, we will still owe about twenty-five thousand."

"We can do this, Mom. Let me help." Gina pulled the five thousand dollar check out of her purse. "I just received this retainer from my client. And there's more to come." She didn't bother to tell her mother that the 'more to come' was contingent on the conversation she had with David later in the week. That didn't matter, because she had gotten her client on one of the hottest cooking shows on television. He won and would continue to be on the show. So, Gina was going to leverage that success to get other clients. She would come up with the money her parents needed, period.

Her mom smiled as she looked at the check, but then she said, "You need that money to pay for your car?"

Gina wished she hadn't told her mother about the car being repossessed. But she had needed that ride to get to Toya's wedding, and she didn't want to lie to her mother in order to get the car. She was just thankful that she hadn't informed her mother about the eviction notice that had been taped to her door after the wedding. "I'm behind by three payments, Mom. That's fifteen hundred dollars. I can pay that and still have money to put down on Dad's hospital bills. So, please let me help."

Audrey shook her head. "What if more money doesn't come in time and you not only lose your car but your apartment. Your father and I would feel awful if we destroyed your good name."

Gina wanted to scream. "Listen to me, Mom. I have already decided to move out of my apartment. I knew you and Daddy wouldn't let me help if I had other bills that I was responsible for, so I'm going to pay my last rent payment and then turn in my notice." Gina stood up and waved her hand around the living room. "You've always said that as long as you have a home, I do too. Well, you and Daddy need to realize that I grew up in this house and that means something to me. I don't want you to just sell it off. One day I will have children, don't you think they'd like them to see the home I grew up in?"

Tears filled Audrey's eyes. She hung her head. "We aren't trying to take away your memories, Gina. I love this house just as much as you did. But we know you don't want this house, so we just wanted to make sure we weren't leaving bills on you."

Gina sat back down next to her mom. She wiped the tears from her eyes. "Don't cry, Mama. I didn't mean to make you cry."

"I'm okay, hon. I just get emotional when thinking about leaving a place I've called home for almost thirty years. We finally paid off the mortgage two years ago. George and I were so happy that he took me out for a steak dinner."

"I remember. You called to tell me about it. You were so excited about growing old in this house. I, of course, thought you sounded a bit morbid. Talking about growing old and even being buried in the back yard."

Audrey smiled at that. "Your father went on and on about the kind of shovel he wanted us to use when digging up his backyard. I tried to ignore him. We had scrimped and saved for one thing or another for so long that I was just happy to be getting a steak dinner at a five-star restaurant."

"See, that's what I mean. How can the two of you go from wanting to live here forever, to 'let's sell the house'?"

"Life has a way of interrupting plans," Audrey wisely answered.

Gina knew that all too well. Life had certainly happened to her ever since she went down that slippery slope of forgetting how she was raised and decided to move in with a man she thought loved her. Now she knew for certain that nothing was worth walking away from the love of God.

"Mom, let me ask you something. Why do you think God gives people children?"

Audrey put a hand under Gina's chin and joyfully squeezed it. "So that they would come to know unconditional love. Having children helps us to understand, in some small way, God's unconditional love for us."

"Yes, I definitely agree with that. But haven't you noticed the number of parents that end up living with their children when they can no longer take care of themselves?"

"Noticed? I was one of them. As you well know, I took care of my mother when she became too ill to take care of herself."

"Did you ever regret helping your mother in her time of need?"

"Of course not, I'd give anything to have the opportunity to do it again."

"So, why are you denying me the chance to help you in your time of need? I know you don't want to sell this house with all its memories. Why even the room we are sitting in holds special memories for you. Because as I remember it, we didn't even have a living room for three years while I was in middle school because

Nana's hospital bed and all the equipment she needed to be able to stay in our home was in this room."

Audrey didn't say anything, she just allowed her eyes to drift around the room as if she was reliving those moments in time when she had been gifted three more years with her mother.

"I know I'm hitting below the belt here," Gina prefaced, "But Nana wouldn't want you to sell a house you love that has so many memories in it either."

"Are you trying to make me cry again?"

"No, please don't do that. I'm trying to help my parents in their time of need. That's all I want to do. This isn't the same way you helped Nana, but it's the way that I can help out. Let me do this for you."

Audrey held up her hands in surrender. "I'll talk to your father."

"Thank you." Gina hugged her mother. "Tell him that if he won't accept my money to pay for the hospital bill, then I'll just buy the house myself, and I'll never move out. How about that?"

The surgery took two hours. Her father was in recovering for about an hour and a half before they were allowed to see him. But the doctor came into the waiting room and informed them that the surgery was successful.

"Thank You, Lord. Oh, what a mighty God we serve," Audrey said as she and Gina hugged and then headed toward the ICU room.

George Melson's eyes fluttered open as Gina and Audrey stood at the side of his bed. "Daddy, you're woke!"

Slowly his eyes closed again. "Let's sit down," Audrey told her daughter. "It may be a while before the meds wear off."

It was a full hour later when George opened his eyes again. His voice was hoarse as he called for his wife, "Audrey, baby, you here?"

Gina stood and walked back to the bed. "Mom, just went to the bathroom, Daddy. She'll be right back. How are you feeling?"

"Like a truck ran over me, then backed up and ran me down again."

"Well, you did just endure a two-hour surgery. But if you think you need some pain meds, I'll put a call in to the nurse."

He nodded, accepting the help as his head fell back against the pillow.

Gina pushed the button for the nurse. "Can I help you?" The woman asked through the intercom.

"Yes, my father is in pain."

"I'll be right there."

Gina placed a hand on her father's arm. "The nurse will be in to take care of the pain."

"He's in pain?" Audrey pushed past Gina until she was in front of her husband. She reached into the bed and grabbed hold of his hand. "How are you feeling, baby? What can I do?"

"Calm down, my love." His voice was still hoarse and low.

Gina watched her parents gaze into each other's eyes. They were silent, but their love spoke volumes. This was the kind of love she wanted. Not some love that ran hot in the beginning and then fizzled out. She wanted a love that could weather the storms of life, survive forty years of disagreements and misunderstandings, survive scrimping and saving, putting a kid through college, and sickness and health and still come through it, gazing lovingly into each other's eyes.

The nurse entered the room. "Well, I guess our patient is awake," she said.

Audrey turned toward the nurse. "He's woke, but he's in pain. Can you help him?"

The nurse pointed to a button that was connected to a bag full of liquid. Her dad's IV was connected to the bag. "This is your pain medicine, sir. Just push this button whenever you feel pain, and it should ease it for you. Give it a try." She put the button in George's hand.

George squeezed the button; within moments, the pain that had been etched on his face subsided and he got this silly grin on his face.

"Your husband is on drugs, Mom," Gina joked.

"He better not get hooked on that stuff. Ain't nothing worse than an old junkie," Audrey said, then shook her head.

The nurse assured them, "He'll be okay. Trust me, we won't let him receive his pain medicine in this manner for too long."

As the nurse walked out of the room, Gina had a thought. Looking down at her father, she said, "Hey Dad, I'm going to take care of your hospital bill, so you don't have to sell the house. Okay?"

"Yes, sure. Thank you, baby girl." George's head bobbed from side to side, then he fell back to sleep.

8

Two days after her father's successful surgery, Gina drove back to Ann Arbor to meet with David. She was no longer driving her mother's Camry because she was able to pay the late payments and get her BMW back. She was happy that she was able to pay the fees on her red beamer, but life had interrupted her need for a luxury car. So, when she picked her car up, she also went to the hardware store and purchased a For Sale sign.

If she was going to stop her parents from selling their home, show them that she was serious about getting that hospital bill paid. Having a five hundred dollars a month car payment would be a hindrance to her goals, so the car had to go. Gina never thought in a million years that giving up her BMW would have been such an easy decision. But once it had been taken, she realized the money spent on her fabulous car could be put to better use.

When she arrived at the restaurant, Gina was surprised to see David standing outside as if he was waiting on her. He opened her door and held out a hand to help her up. "Thank you."

"You're welcome. How is your father?"

Wow, he got two points for that. She was here for a business meeting, but the first thing David wanted to know was how her father was doing. "Much better. The surgery was successful. If all goes well, they will be taking him off oxygen soon. Once they do that, then we'll know for sure if his quality of life will be any better."

"Let me know if I can do anything."

"Thanks for that, David, but we're just in wait and see mode right now."

As they headed into the restaurant, he pointed at the sign in her back window. "You're selling your whip?"

Gina nodded, then quickly changed the subject. "Where do you want to have our conversation. Are we going to be sitting at a booth or do you have an office in the back so we can speak privately?"

"I've already taken the liberty to set some things up for us in my office. Follow me, Ms. Gina."

As she stepped into David's office, Gina was surprised to see a small round table with seating for two in the middle of the room and a six-foot table against the wall with more food than she and David could eat in the space of three meetings. "You don't mess around."

"I know that you liked our BLT, so we have that here." He pointed to the delicious sandwich. "But I wanted you to try a few other items that we have on the menu, so I've given us sample portions of some of the menu items."

"If you're trying to butter me up," Gina picked up a plate and started placing items on it, "It's working." She spotted a dip with chips but couldn't make out what kind of dip it was. Pointing towards it, she asked, "What's that?"

"That's my Wild Bill Buffalo dip."

"I saw a picture on the wall of someone named Bill Hoffman, is he the one you named this dip after?" Gina knew that there was a story behind each one of David's creations. She couldn't wait to hear this one.

"Yep, you guessed it. Bill was a three-hundred-pound linebacker who played for the Buffalo Bills. That guy tried to knock my head off every time we played against them. It became my goal in life to run as fast as I could so Wild Bill couldn't tackle me."

"You must've hated him," Gina said as she added some salad to her plate.

"Believe it or not, he's now one of my best friends."

Laughing, Gina told him. "That's crazy. If he had sat his big self on me, I probably wouldn't speak to him for the rest of my life."

They sat down at the table. David said, "Don't you attend Christ Life withe Toya and Jarrod?"

"Yes, sir, I certainly do. And we have the best pastors in the world, who also happen to be Toya's mother and Jarrod's father."

"Weird how that happened, huh?" Before waiting for her response, he asked, "Don't they teach forgiveness over at Christ Life?"

"Hey," she protested. "I'm a forgiving person. I just don't like people messing with me."

"Isn't that the point of forgiving… the person messed with you in some way, and instead of hating on them, you do what the Bible instructs."

Gina avoided eye contact with David and started eating her food because she didn't have an answer to his question. In truth, someone had in fact, messed with her, and even though she truly loved God, she still hadn't been able to forgive. So, what did that say about her? "Mmmh, my God, this is good. Have you always been able to cook like this?"

"Since I was a boy in my grandmother's kitchen. Nana taught me well. After football, I went to culinary school and learned a few other techniques."

"I didn't get that cooking gene from my grandmother nor my mother. I mostly just sat in the kitchen for moral support."

"What? You can't cook? How do you feed yourself?"

"Takeout. And I hope you're going to let me take some of this food home with me."

"That depends on how our meeting goes?" David joked.

But his comment brought Gina back to reality. She was here for a purpose, so she needed to get down to business. But the mac and cheese on her plate was calling for her. She took a few more bites then put down her fork. "First, I want to thank you for giving me this assignment. I have been praying and sending out proposals in order to get new clients, and I'm just grateful for this opportunity."

"But…"

"But, I'm concerned about what Katie told me."

David slid his chair back; his body went stiff. "What concerns you?"

His body language told her that he wasn't happy to be talking about this at all. But she had to make sure she wasn't working for a monster. "The thing is, the details of what happened to your accuser are awful. And to be honest with you, I don't think I could respect nor work with a man who could do something like that to a woman. So, I really need to know the truth about the situation."

"And the reason it concerned you is that you think I'm the kind of guy who would do something like that, right?"

"No, actually, I have always thought of you as the pretend-to-love-'em and then leave-'em kind of guy. I would have never pegged you as an abuser. I want to believe you didn't do it, but then I'm reminded of that Panthers football player who had his girlfriend killed because she was pregnant, and he didn't want to pay child support. So, it does happen."

David pounded the table with his fist. "It doesn't happen with me. That's not who I am!"

"Then why is this woman blackmailing you? Why would she accuse you of such a thing with no reason?"

"I wish I knew." David jerked away from the table as he stood up. He paced the floor like a grizzly marking his territory. "I only went out with her a couple of times. I thought things were going good. I actually thought we hit it off, I had even been thinking about taking our relationship to the next level. The next thing I knew she showed up at my office in Dallas and told Katie that I beat her."

"Wait… wait. You just skipped over something very important. When did you find out about the baby?"

David shook his head and his hands at the same time. "She never told me anything about a baby. But the hospital records she gave to Katie showed that she had indeed lost a baby. But it wasn't mine."

"How can you be so sure. I mean, you were dating her, correct?" If Gina knew anything about David Pittman is was that he was fond of the ladies and made his move quick. And then, of course, he forgot he ever knew them.

"And my dating her means I obviously must have slept with her, right?"

"Well yeah." He sounded so angry. But Gina didn't understand his anger, that had been his MO. Not just in college, because she also remembered reading about his exploits while playing professional ball.

"I have been celibate for the past two years." He sat back down at the table, slumped in his seat and stared at her.

Gina was taking a sip of her tea. She almost choked on it and had to spit it out. "I'm sorry." She took a napkin and tipped her mouth and the table. "Excuse me? What did you just say?"

"You heard me."

"But did I hear you right? Did you really just tell me that you gave up sex two years ago?" Her mouth hung open as she waited for a response.

He just nodded.

"And you're not lying?" She just couldn't believe this.

"I gave up lying and drinking too," he told her matter-of-factly.

She could hardly believe what she was hearing. The only people she knew who willingly gave up sex, lying and drinking were Christians. "Wait... are you saved?"

David doubled over laughing. As he laughed, he pointed at her and laughed some more.

"What's so funny?"

"Wait... wait... wait." He tried to stop laughing, as he said, "You should have seen your face. Like you couldn't believe that God would want to 'save' me." He lifted his hands and shook his fingers as if giving praise to God when he said the word 'save'.

"I never said that."

"Oh, but it was implied." David tsk-tsked at her, then said, "Growing up, I never fully understood what the church folk meant when they said that this person or that person was saved. I always wanted to know, saved from what? I can't tell you how many times I asked my grandmother about that." Looking off as if thinking about a distant memory, one that made him smile, "She would say, 'saved from the world. Now, go somewhere and play, boy'."

"You grew up in church?"

"I wouldn't say I grew up in church because my mom and dad were more like Christmas and Easter churchgoers until about ten years ago. But I spent weekends with my grandmother a couple times a month, that's when I went to church. Grandma Patty taught me a lot about the Bible. I could even recite all sixty-six books of the Bible by the time I was fifteen."

"Wow! That's quite an accomplishment. I wouldn't be able to recite all those books if someone offered to pay me. Shame."

"Genesis, Exodus, Leviticus, Number, Deuteronomy…"

"Okay, okay, you don't have to be a showoff," Gina interrupted him. "We will just make a note that you are good at everything. A true renaissance man."

"Well, you know, what can I say." He flexed his muscles, showing off biceps and triceps.

The man certainly hadn't gone to flab after hanging up his cleats, that's for sure. Gina was actually enjoying her time with David, and from the exchange they had at the wedding, she really didn't think it would be possible to enjoy spending time with a man like David. But maybe, she needed to readjust the way she thought of David because clearly, he was not the same immature guy she met back in college. "So, what changed?"

With a raised eyebrow, David said, "I'm not sure what you mean?"

"Well, you were obviously a grandmama's boy, in the kitchen cooking with her, going to church and learning the books of the Bible for her. But you didn't seem anything like that in college."

Lifting a finger to correct her, he said, "I was still a grandmama's boy until the day Grandma Patty went home to be with the Lord, and I do sometimes feel her presence when I'm in the kitchen whipping up a new creation. But to be honest with you, I did lose a piece of myself and it started in college.

"I had my first drink during my freshmen year, and it was downhill from there. I would have blackouts and do outrageous things while drinking." He turned and looked directly into Gina's eyes. "Do you want to know why it was so important that I attend Jarrod's wedding even though this messy situation had just reared its ugly head?"

"Yes, I think I would like to know." Gina was seeing another side of David. A side that she was really beginning to enjoy hanging out with.

"Since I was this big-time football superstar," lifting his hands, he put 'superstar' in air quotation marks "I got away with a lot of bad behavior. But the moment I wasn't running down the field with that football and scoring the winning touchdown for my team, my behavior was no longer acceptable. But, I didn't know how to stop being who I had become. I'd get drunk and get into fights, get thrown out of bars. I'd wake up with some woman I didn't remember, that was awkward.

"Then, each time I tried to re-enter this world I thought I knew I kept getting rejected. It was no to a coaching job, no to a TV analysis job, it was painful, but I took the blows and kept drinking. Until one day, I found myself at my grandmother's funeral so drunk that my mother had the ushers throw me out of the church. I sat on the church steps crying like a baby. Because I wanted to change but I didn't know how."

Gina couldn't believe what she was hearing. People think the rich have it made, but David truly struggled to find his way. She didn't tell him any of her thoughts because she didn't want to interrupt the story.

He continued, "While on those steps, the door of the church opened. Jarrod walked out and came to sit next to me. I hadn't seen him in years. The only thing I'd ever done was send him free tickets to games when we were playing anywhere close to Michigan, and he never asked for anything more."

"Jarrod's a good guy," Gina said.

"He's one of the best," David agreed. "I don't know how he found out about my grandmother's death, but he came to see about me because he knew what that woman meant to me. That's the day that life began to make sense to me. He told me that he'd been praying for me. I don't remember all his words that day because I was wasted. But I remember us praying together and I remembering calling on Jesus and asking Him to be my savior. So, yes, Gina, I am saved. I'm blood bought. I was even baptized again. All thanks to Jarrod, so I wasn't about to miss his wedding."

When he finished speaking, Gina nodded. "I believe you. But now we need to figure out why this woman would lie on you before she stirs up more trouble and costs you this cooking show."

"She's already stirring up more trouble." David showed Gina a text message on his phone. "She's threatening to go to the media."

9

The text message read: "I guess you think I'm playing with yo' black behind. But I will put you on blast. CNN and our local news station are just a phone call away."

"She doesn't mention anything about money in that text. Nor does she say anything about what she wants. Are you just supposed to guess?" Gina asked.

"She already told Katie that she wanted two million. I don't think she wants to put that in writing for fear that I might show it to the police."

"And the sad thing about it is if she really had been hurt the way she claimed, you'd think she would have gone to the police rather than trying to get money out of you." As she said those words, she was reminded of the day she had gone to the ER because she'd been beaten. She hadn't reported Marvel to the police either, but that was because she was terrified of the man. As she endured the pain from her broken arm, she plotted how she could escape to a place where Marvel wouldn't find her.

"The thing that gets me is I was finally a gentleman with a woman. I didn't try to kiss her, to get her in bed, none of that. I took her out on a few dates and really tried to get to know who she was and the things she enjoyed. Then boom, she wants my money for something I didn't do."

Tapping a finger to her chin, Gina tried to think this through until her head hurt. She reached in her purse for the Advil. "We don't need to figure that woman's deal out right now. But we do need to get started on your campaign for The Grind."

"Oh, so I passed your inquisition? You're going to continue working with me?"

"No need to rub it in. I shouldn't have pre-judged you; I apologize for that." She took her Advil and then held out a hand to him. "Truce?"

He shook her hand. "Truce."

Getting down to business, she pulled out her notepad and pen. "Tell me why you picked Alzheimer as the charity you want to represent?"

"Oh, that's easy. My dad. He always seemed so strong to me. Best man I ever met. When Alzheimer hit, it broke my heart. I'd give anything to find a cure for this disease."

"Oooh, that was good." Gina jotted down a few notes. "Say it just like that when the judges ask you about it."

He gave her the hand on that comment. "Are you suggesting that I use my father's illness to advance my career?"

Looking a little sheepish, she told him, "It sounds bad when you put it that way. But you're the one who picked Alzheimer's because it's something you're passionate about. And the charity you highlight on The Grind should be something you're passionate about. They will ask you why you picked that charity, so you need to be comfortable talking about your father and relate him to this illness."

"I haven't been comfortable with this thing called Alzheimer since it zapped the life my father used to know right out of his head."

"Keep in mind that half of that fifty thousand dollars prize will go to the winner's charity. That money could do a lot of good. It may not help your father, but think of other families that might not have to deal with what you all have if more research could be done or more marketing to at-risk families."

"I hear you. Basically, I'm just being selfish."

"I wouldn't call you selfish. This issue hits hard. But you've hired me to help build your brand nationally. And I am giving you my professional opinion, which is, if Alzheimer is your charity then you have to talk about your father. I even think we should get some live shots with you and your father and have them aired on the show. You want to win, then this is what we have to do. Or you can pick a different charity."

Leaning back in his seat again, David stared at Gina for a long moment. "You don't believe in sugar-coating it for a brother, do you?"

Scrunching her nose, she shook her head. "I've always been a straight shooter. I have to tell it like it is, in as few words as possible. Can you work with someone like me?"

"As long as you have my best interest and my family's best interest in mind, then I can work with you."

"Trust me, David. I would never do anything that would hurt you or your father. If you allow us to highlight him for The Grind, I promise it will be done in the most tasteful manner that allows him to hold onto his dignity. Because I know how hard it is when parents get ill and can't help themselves anymore. I'm selling my car so I can pay my father's hospital bills and keep them in my childhood home. So, I get it."

He looked at her as if he finally saw her. "You do get it, don't you?"

~~~

David was mesmerized by Gina. She handled her business and still managed to think of others. In his world, the type of women he ran into wanted him to buy them a luxury car, they weren't selling their car to help their parents with hospital bills.

His friends only ran into gold-digging women too. But he guessed that was the nature of the beast. When women saw athletes, they saw dollar signs, they saw an instant monthly check for eighteen years. David was only thankful that he'd never been trapped into that baby mama drama. But his friend Bill hadn't been so lucky. He was paying child support for five kids by three different baby mamas and they were constantly going back and forth to court trying to up his support even though he was paying about two thousand a month for each kid.

"I love my kids, but these women." Bill shook his head. "They trying to drain me."

David was at his restaurant in Ann Arbor again with Bill. He hadn't seen his buddy in a few months and was happy to catch up with him, but he didn't have much sympathy for the situation. "You should have kept them pants on and you wouldn't be shelling out money like you Bank of America or something. Them women don't even care that you ain't bringing in bank like that no more."

"Tell me about it. My youngest child's mama asked the judge to make me go back to football. Like I wouldn't still be playing if I hadn't broken both my knees and my right foot. I'm walking around with so many replacement parts that I get pulled aside at the airport on the regular."

They both laughed at that. Then David said, "That's what you get. Yo' three hundred pound self was always putting your full weight on people. That's why them knees kept hitting the ground."

"That was my job, and I did it well. But I don't deserve what these women are doing to me. My ex-wife is trying to get her hands on my pension, so once I'm done paying her child support and I'm finally able to collect my pension, she'll be getting part of that."

"Word? I didn't know these women could get hold of the pension. I thought she still had to be married to you."

Bill rolled his eyes, "My dumb self stayed married to the Wicked-One," his term of endearment for his ex and the mother of his first two children, "for ten years, which apparently might be all she needs to lay her grubby hands on my pension."

"See, stuff like that makes me glad I'm celibate."

"Celi-what?"

"You heard me, I'm celibate and have been for the past two years."

Bill turned, looking around the restaurant. Then he turned back to David with a look of astonishment on his face. "How come I'm just now hearing about this?"

"It's not something that I shout to the world. But I take my faith seriously and have decided to honor God by waiting until I find a woman to marry before I have sex again. Besides, I've been there, done that, and have had enough sex for three lifetimes already. I can wait and do things right this time."

"My man." Bill raised his glass of ice-tea in salute, he laughed a bit, took a sip of his tea. "No wonder you told me I should keep my pants on, you been doing it now for two years. I'm impressed."

"Well, don't be. It's just my personal conviction. But you know what, I think it's helped me. Since I stopped focusing so much on what woman I could get in bed, I was able to focus on my career. I finished culinary school and opened two restaurants. God has been good."

"Maybe I need to try being celibate or something. Maybe I'd be able to focus on my next move. Because I'm running out of dough."

David nodded. "That was a bad break with the NFL making you pay part of that signing bonus. I mean, it's their fault you couldn't perform on that field anymore."

"Thank you!" Bill blurted out the words so loud that a few customers turned and stared. He waved at the pretty olive complexion woman two tables over, then winked at her.

"See, you haven't learned nothing. Have a baby with that one and see what happens."

"Shut up, man, I was just flirting. Besides, I'm not trying to have no more kids. I'm a retired man... and even that still burns me. The only reason I retired was because my team was about to cut me while I was on injured reserve. After all the years I spent in the league, I earned the respect of retiring rather than being cut, like I hadn't given nothing to this game. But the minute I retired they came after my money. That ain't right."

All David could do was shake his head. Because he had retired at the end of his contract, so the league didn't come after him for any of his money. He had been able to reset his life by opening the restaurants, but Bill has endured one problem after the next. A lot of guys go broke within a few years of leaving the NFL. Mostly due to the reckless way they live when the money is pouring in like rain. Nobody ever expects the rain to stop. And when it does, the mortgage is still due, the kids still need new shoes and the women are still coming after that money. "Have you thought about what you can do to bring in some more money?" His friend had never spoken of any other interests outside of football.

"Man, I've been racking my brain on that one. My family never encouraged me to do nothing but tackle the guy in front of me. They told me football would save me. But look at me now. I'm just glad I had sense enough to pay off my mama's house and put it in her name. At least I've got a place to lay my head if all else fails."

"I hear you, man, and I'll be praying for you." Bill didn't respond to that. But David got the feeling that he wasn't much interested in prayers. His friend just didn't know that it was a prayer that changed everything for him. One simple prayer and a man named Jesus. David prayed that he would soon be able to truly introduce that man to his friend.

10

Publicity opportunities were rolling in. David was the bad boy who'd picked himself up and done well. People were suckers for those kinds of stories. The Alzheimer angle was good also. Because it showed that even though he had been a big-time superstar football player, he still cared about others. Gina had booked him on Good Morning America so he could chat it up with Michael Strahan about the good old days of football and then show off his cooking skills with Robin Roberts.

He was a guest on the Steve Harvey Morning Radio show, which is run out of Los Angeles. David did not want to fly to LA so Gina was able to get a call-in for him. The woman had been doing an awesome job and he couldn't be happier that he hired her. She had been booking national tv spots and syndicated radio for him. If he did a local event, she always made sure that he received social media and news coverage. Now she was trying to convince him to do an event for Alzheimer's.

It wasn't like he hadn't wanted to do something to raise awareness and bring funds into the organization, but he'd been hesitant to talk about Alzheimer's. Naming it as his charity, was one thing, but opening up and letting people know about his real-life situation was something altogether different.

Before making the decision to do the event, he drove to Detroit to meet with Gina. He needed her to understand why he was hesitant. He knocked on her door and waited. When she opened the door, he held up the white bags he had in both hands.

"Is that food from the restaurant?" She rubbed her hands together.

"Girl, you greedy." He stepped inside her apartment.

"You're the one who keeps feeding me. What you want me to do? Turn down good food. Not in this lifetime." She reached for one of the bags.

He held onto it as he glanced around the room. "You moving?" She had boxes stacked in the living room.

She turned and looked at the boxes. "Oh yeah, I'm making steady progress. We can sit in the kitchen and talk if it's too cluttered in here for you."

He followed her to the kitchen. He put the bags on the counter. "Whatcha got?" Gina asked as she helped him empty the bags.

"Sandwiches and Gumbo. I'm trying out a recipe that I want to name after my father."

"So why is this gumbo being named after your dad?"

"His people are from New Orleans. So it's kind of my way of respecting those roots."

As they sat down to eat, Gina got down to business, discussing the upcoming Alzheimer events that she planned for him in Dallas. She also asked about his hesitancy to do the events.

That's when he confided in her, "I never thought that I would have to put either of my parents in a home. But my mom said that he kept running off, and she was terrified that he would harm himself."

"So, you did what was best for your father, right?" Gina asked.

"Yes, of course, my mother loves my father. It breaks her heart that he can't be at home with her. And if I didn't travel and work so much, I would have him with me."

"Again, you did what was best for your father, right?"

An eyebrow went up. "Why do you keep asking me that?"

"Because I want you to get it through your head that you have nothing to be ashamed of. Don't you dare blame yourself for something that happened to your dad that you had no control over."

"I know I had no control over it. I didn't do this to him, football did it as far as I'm concerned." David voiced raised, then he lowered it.

"But you still blame yourself. I hear it in the way you talk about it," Gina wasn't letting up.

"I wouldn't say I blame myself. I just feel bad that I can't take care of him the way he always took care of me."

She leaned closer to him and put a hand on his arm. "You love your father; I know that and anyone who talks to you will know that. Be at peace with your decision and stop beating yourself up."

That hand of Gina's had magic powers or something because he instantly felt like heat radiated up his arm and through his entire body when she touched him. Her mere presence brought him comfort. "How are you able to do that?"

"What did I do?"

"You help me to look at things so differently. There's no other way to explain how I feel except to say I feel comforted around you."

Smiling, she said, "Since you and I are going to be working together for a little while, I'm glad to know you're comforted by my presence. Especially since you didn't even want me around in the beginning."

"That's because you run that mouth too much sometimes," he told her good naturedly.

Gina shoved him. "I do not run my mouth. I speak up when something needs to be said. That's called being assertive."

"No, that's called being a pain in the neck," But for all his bluster, he knew she was right. And in truth, his mother simply couldn't keep his father at the house any longer. The whole family had worked out a plan and had agreed that the best thing for him was to be in a facility where he could receive round the clock care. And David made sure his father was in the best facility and that quality people were caring for him.

He visited his father at least once, sometimes twice a month. David told her that the visits went well when his father remembered him, but when he didn't, the rest of the week was all bad for David. He hated seeing his father like this. Football had given so much to him over the years but it had also taken from him. Although his father never played pro-ball, he had played football since he was six years old, then played in high school. He suffered a concussion. Played in college, suffered several concussions and a broken leg. So, he never made it to the pros, but he made sure that his son went all the way. It was just sad now that his father couldn't even remember any of it most of the time.

They traveled to Dallas to do the events that Gina had on his schedule. David's mom had made it out to the Alzheimer's Walk-a-Thon, and she and David partnered up for the walk to earn money for Alzheimer's. The event was posted on Twitter, Instagram and his Facebook page. People were invited to donate to the Alzheimer's organization with a link to make the donation. At the end of the walk, David and his mom sat down with a local newspaper and a local news station for an interview.

David felt that some good had been done for the cause of Alzheimer's that day. He was in such a good mood that when the event was over, he called a 5-star seafood restaurant in the area and made reservations. Then he walked over to where Gina and his mother stood, positioned himself in-between them and then put an arm around both women. "How about I take my two best girls to get some seafood?"

~~~

Gina was caught off guard by David saying that she and his mother were his two best girls. His mother gave her the side-eye like she was some fortune hunter scheming her way into David's pockets.

Gina extracted herself from David's arm. "You go with your mother. I'm sure the two of you have a lot to talk about. I can grab a bite and catch an Uber to the hotel."

"No way, Gina, we aren't letting you pick up some fast food sandwich and eat by yourself while we dine on seafood. You're the reason we're here anyway."

Gina shook her head. "I don't want to intrude. Your mother hasn't been able to spend much time with you today because we've been so busy."

David turned to his mother, "Mama, will you please tell Gina that she is more than welcome to have dinner with us?"

Mary turned to Gina, the look on her face was pleasant as she said, "David is right, Dear. You flew all the way to Dallas to help us with this event, it wouldn't be right for us to let you go off by yourself. If my son hadn't made reservations already, I would have taken you home and fed you."

Gina wasn't sure if Mary really meant what she was saying or if she didn't want to be rude. But there was no way she'd be able to decline now "Mrs. Mary, you are so sweet. I'd love to have dinner with you and your son. Thank you."

"No need to thank me, my son is paying. And if I know him, this restaurant is going to be top-notch. But you deserve it. I really think we did some good for our cause today," Mary told her.

"We did. At the next event, I'd love to have your husband join us if that's alright with you," she broached the subject as gently as possible with Mary, hoping that the woman wouldn't object.

"That would be lovely. Thank you for including my Davie." She hugged Gina before getting in David's car. "I had a good feeling about you when we met this morning. You've got a good heart, Gina."

"Thank you for saying that, Mrs. Mary."

"Stop calling me Mrs. Mary. I'm just Mary."

"Okay." Gina got in the back seat while Mary sat in the front next to her son.

"Now, Gina, what are you planning to do with the photos and videos that were taken today?" Mary asked.

"I'm creating a package to send to The Grind. They will use as much or as little of it as they see fit. I'll have video editors working on the final product because we want to make sure that we send the show really good footage."

"I'm not going to be edited out, am I? I love that show, and a lot of my friends on the Mother's board at church watch it, so if I tell them I'll be on it, I don't want to look like a liar."

"I will do my best to make sure you don't get edited out, Mary. I promise."

"Gina's good at her job, Mama. So, don't worry. She'll find a way to work you in."

"She better. Because I don't want to look like a fool spouting off about The Grind and how I'm making a cameo appearance, and once again, it's just my famous son. I mean, no offense Junior, but your mug has been seen all over the place. It's time for mama to shine."

"Mama, you shine all the time," David told her.

Mary turned toward the back and addressed Gina. "I'm not just being some prima donna either. Junior has owed me this for ten years, and he knows it."

"Not that again, Mama. Will you please give it a rest." David pulled up to the valet area. He hopped out of the car and handed the valet his keys, then opened the door for Gina while the valet opened the door for his mother. Ladies, shall we?" He put an arm out for his mother and Gina to loop their arms into, then they walked into the restaurant arm and arm.

Gina was mesmerized the moment they walked into the restaurant. This was no ordinary seafood place. It was dimly lit with chandeliers hanging above most of the tables, the waiters wore tailored suits and the hostess wore a designer dress that most waitresses would have to save two months worth of salary for. She felt uncomfortable as the three of them waited to be seated in their walk-a-thon t-shirt. Gina thought the hostess would for sure tell David he needed a jacket on. It was that kind of place.

But after David gave them his name and she made a note of his reservation, she was very pleasant as she showed them to their table. When the waiter brought the menus, Gina opened hers, she wanted to close it shut, run out of this place and go find a Captain D's for some fish and chips because that's the kind of budget she was dealing with. She told David, "This place is too expensive. I wouldn't feel right having you pay for my meal in here."

David shook his head. "You are too much, Gina Melson."

"No," she pointed at the menu. "This place is too much. I bet you a glass of water is twenty dollars."

Mary opened her menu. "You're wrong, Gina. The water is twenty-five dollars."

Mary and Gina giggled.

"Will you two stop, you're making me look bad. And trust me, I'm not going to go broke after picking up the tab for dinner tonight. So, please order whatever you like. It's on me, and I'm happy to do it."

"Okay, if you say so." Gina started examining her menu again. The shrimp scampi looked good, but the pasta sounded good also. She didn't want to deal with crab legs because that just took too much energy. Oh, but she did love crab cakes and they had them on the menu. She was putting her menu down as she had found what she wanted when a woman dressed in a form-fitting sweater dress with the most fabulous white boots Gina had ever seen. The boots strapped all the way up to the knee, with white fur covering the top of the boot and rhinestones cascaded down the front of the boot.

"Hey, handsome," the woman said as she approached the table.

David had a silly grin on his face as he turned toward the woman. Once recognizing her, he stood and pulled her into an embrace. "Sheila Maddox, I thought you fell off the face of the earth. How you've been?" David glanced around the room. "And where's that husband of yours?"

Sheila scrunched her nose as if the mention of her husband caused her to smell something foul. "We aren't together anymore, I let that loser go."

"Phil Maddox was one of the finest men I have ever had the privilege of playing pro-ball with. He is far from a loser," he told the woman.

"Yeah, okay, you knew him before he became best friends with Jack Daniels."

He turned his shoulder away from her as he said, "Let me introduce you, Sheila." David pointed toward Mary, "This is my mom, Mary Pittman." He then pointed toward Gina. "And this is Gina Melson, my publicist."

"That's a bold move, coming in here all casual like that, Gina."

Gina's eyelashes fluttered several times, but she managed to keep her mouth shut.

Sheila then turned to David's mom and extended a hand, "Hello Mary, I'm an old friend of David's."

Mary shook the woman's hand, then added, "It's Mrs. Pittman, dear."

Now Sheila's eyelashes fluttered. She stepped back as if she'd been slapped.

David gave his mother the eye and then asked Sheila, "Do you have a number,"

Quickly reaching into her purse, Sheila said, "I certainly do, Boo."

"Where I can contact Phil?"

Sheila would not be a good poker player. She twirled her hair, sucked her teeth again as she rolled her eyes. "What? You gon' call and ask him to send my child support? If not, you're better off calling me."

Gina couldn't take any more of this woman. She leaned over and whispered to Mary. "You want to tell me about the media event that went wrong ten years ago… the reason David owes you for this one?"

Mary shook her head. "I sound like a diva. I never should have brought it up."

Gina could see Sheila handing David a piece of paper out of the periphery of her eye. Ignoring them, she said to Mary, "You're not being a diva. And if that incident was important to you back then, it will be important to me now."

David sat back down as Sheila strutted off. He then butted into their conversation. "I'll tell you why my mom feels like she's been ignored by the media."

Gina was irritated with David, so she told him, "I'd rather hear it from Mary if you don't mind."

Smirking, as she looked from her son to Gina, Mary said, "Well, what had happened was… I got all dressed up for this media event Junior told me he was doing that would involve the family. I thought we were all going to sit on the sofa and chat about Junior, but the reporter decided to sit three chairs in the middle of the room. He put me in the third chair and let Junior's daddy sit in the middle. They acted like I wasn't even there, the reporter only asked questions of my husband and Junior. When the piece aired, they had even cut me out of most of the interview. See, I wasn't needed since I wasn't talking."

"Oh, wow, I'm so sorry that happened to you," Gina said.

"Me too, because she's never let me forget it," David said.

Mary put a hand on David's arm and sighed. "Your dad started losing his memory a couple years after that. So, believe it or not, I watch that interview ever now and then just to remind me of the man I once knew. I don't have anything to complain about, Junior. That interview went exactly how it should have."

11

She heard the words Mary said out of her mouth, but Gina thought there might still be something in her heart about an incident that occurred over ten years ago. So Gina made sure that Mary was included in each and every interview David did the following day. The last stop was at the nursing home. As they walked in, Gina caught a whiff of the distinct old people's smell. It was off-putting because she first assumed she was smelling urine, but then remembered one of her first public relations assignments was with a retirement/assisted living home. The first thing Gina advised them to do was to do something with the smell, the owner then informed her that what she was smelling was a body order that comes from older people.

"As much as you pay for your father to stay in this place, you'd think they'd do something about the smell," Mary complained.

"There's not much they can do," Gina informed her.

David gave her a questioning glance.

She explained, "My first public relations assignment was to attract more people to this retirement/assisted living community. I discovered at that time that as we get older, our bodies generate this smell, that's typically referred to as 'old people's smell'. But the proper term for it is Nonenal. It's like a musty, grassy smell that attaches itself to our skin as we lose omega-7 acids from our skin."

"I don't have no 'old people's smell," Mary declared, looking a bit indignant.

"Of course you don't, and everybody doesn't get the 'old people's smell'." Gina agreed. "From the research I did on the subject, some people just don't get it, and others avoid it because of their healthy lifestyle of exercise and eating right, you might not develop it. Which obviously you do. I mean, look at you. I can tell that you work out." David's mother wasn't thin as a rail, but she was slim-thick like she lifted weights to keep her muscles toned.

"Gina, I know you're just flattering me because you work for my son, but I don't care." Mary swirled around then struck a pose. "I look good for a sixty-nine-year-old woman."

"Yes, you do," David agreed. "And I can vouch for Gina. She doesn't sugar coat anything for me. She doesn't care that I'm paying her. She will call it like she sees it."

Gina graced Davie with a smile. The man just seemed to get her. "Thank you for saying that, David. I do pride myself on honesty. And Mary, I can honestly say, I think you and I are kindred spirits. I have truly enjoyed hanging out with you this weekend."

"Likewise, Ms. Gina. Now can you tell me how long my husband needs to participate? Some days are good for him, but most days aren't. And I don't want to overexcite him."

"I get it, Mary. We only have one reporter scheduled today. But we are doing national news. So the reporter will interview one of the doctors here who has already agreed to discuss Alzheimer's and the nurse who takes care of your husband. Then we will interview the three of you. And that will be it. So, for now, you can visit with Mr. Pittman and I'll get everything set up."

David grabbed her hand and held on to it. "You can get things set up in a few minutes. I want you to meet my father."

Gina allowed David to guide her down the hallway while still holding her hand. He had seemed nervous from the moment they walked into the nursing home, so she wanted to be there for him when he greeted his father. As he told her before, when his father didn't recognize him, the rest of his week was all bad. This press event had been her bright idea, so the least she could do was hold David's hand and try to reassure him that it was going to be alright.

Mary knocked on her husband's door, then opened it. "Hey, old man, how you doing today?"

David Pittman Senior was seated in a chair with the remote in his hand. There were sprinkles of gray in his hair and beard, but other than that, the man whose brown eyes brightened as he turned toward them looked like an older version of David. The man was not just handsome, he was distinguished.

"Mable is that you. I haven't seen you in a month of Sundays."

Mary's face dropped. "His sister's name is Mable," she told Gina as she walked over to her husband and sat down on the sofa next to his chair.

David Sr. tugged on his jacket. "They put me in this monkey suit because Mary is coming to visit me today. I hope she hurries up so I can get back into my pajamas."

"I'm sure she'll be here soon, David," Mary said as she leaned forward and put a hand over her husband's and squeezed it.

David Jr.'s shoulders slumped as he released Gina's hand. He walked over to his parents and sat down next to his mom. He put an arm around his mother and pulled her close to him.

"I'm okay." Mary stiffened her lip as she raised her chin. "Just let me sit here with him. I'll be okay."

"I hope you'll still be here when Mary comes home. I swear I don't know what takes that woman so long. But she loves that mall. Always coming in with all these new outfits. Junior spoils her, but I love it. I certainly wouldn't have been able to provide for her like that."

"In a way, you did provide for her. Because it was you who spent all those hours working with Junior and making sure he was in the right leagues and the right schools," Mary said, giving him the credit he deserved.

"I sure did. That son of mine was going to be something in this world. You came to his games." David Sr. puffed out his chest. "He was special on that field." David Sr. glanced over at his son and asked, "Now, which one of Mabel's sons are you?"

As if they had played this game a million times with his father, David Junior quickly said, "I'm Joe, the youngest son."

Senior snapped his finger. "That's right. I don't know how I could have forgotten, you look just like my boy."

Gina walked over to David and whispered in his ear, "I need to get the crew started."

David popped out of his seat and backed Gina away from his father. He spoke in a whisper. "I can't have them in here confusing my father and getting him upset."

"I'm not going to do anything to hurt him. Please trust me."

"Who is this lovely lady you have with you, Joe?" Senior asked.

David swung back around to face his father. "Oh, hey, Da… Uncle David, this is my girl, Gina. She's just hanging out with us today."

"Well, you better hold onto that one tight, because if my son comes to see us today, he just might try to steal her from you. Davie loves the pretty ladies."

Gina left the room to make sure that the doctor and nurse who were going to be interviewed knew which conference room they needed to be in, then she waited for the reporter and the camera crew. Once everyone was set, she had a thought and ran out to her rental car. She opened the trunk and pulled out one of the DVDs that she had ordered online and then went back to David Senior's room with it.

The DVD player was already plugged up in the room. She asked David to put the DVD in and let it play.

"What's this?" He asked.

She looked into his eyes, trying to send him a message, hoping that they were connecting. "Trust me, I have a good feeling about this."

He nodded and did as she requested. His father complained as David's back was to him. "Hey, I was watching that movie. You didn't ask me if you could touch my TV. My son bought me that TV."

"I'm sorry, but I've got something I was told you'd want to see." David hit play and then sat back down next to his mother.

"I still didn't say you could touch that TV. I don't allow folks to come in this house touching my stuff," David Senior told him.

As the football game appeared on the screen, Senior stopped fussing and watched the game. After a few minutes, Senior laughed as he pointed at the screen. "I remember that game. They let me stand on the sideline." His eyes lit up as he turned to his wife and son, "Remember that Junior? Your mother got so mad because she was still sitting in the stands while I was cheering for you on the sidelines, just like I used to do when you were in high school."

David leaned forward in his seat. "You remember that game, D-Dad?"

Senior was grinning from ear-to-ear as he looked at his family. "You and I had some good times together, boy." He tapped his head with his index finger. "This ol' mind isn't working like it used to, but somethings I'm just not gon' never forget."

"Yeah, Dad. We had some good times together." David stood and walked over to the door. He wiped his face before turning back around.

"Why you so quiet, Mary? Grab one of them rocking chairs and come sit next to me, woman."

As Mary happily complied with her husband, David walked over to Gina. Gratitude filled his eyes as he hugged. "How did you know? Girl, you got skills."

Gina mimicked what he'd done when she gave him a compliment. She flexed biceps and triceps and strutted around him, "Well, you know, what can I say."

"Okay, smart mouth. What do we do next?"

He was looking at her like she could do no wrong like she had finally won his trust. She didn't want to let him down, so she silently prayed, asking God to direct her path as she lead their family through the last event before they went back to The Grind. But what was most important to Gina was that David Senior held onto his dignity during the interview. So, she was prepared to shut it down if he regressed again.

But everything went smoothly, Senior didn't mind the reporter or the cameraman joining them. He regaled them with stories of his son's wonder years. When the interview began, Gina made sure that Mary was seated in the middle of her son and husband. But even that didn't seem to help, because instead of jumping in and answering questions, Mary seemed content to hang on her husband's every word.

Gina whispered in the reporter's ear, and then he said, "So Mary, what was it like raising a future hall of famer?"

That was all it took and the flood gates were opened. Mary was only too happy to talk about her son. Gina's job was done. With a big sigh of relief, Gina said, "And that's a wrap."

As the cameraman was putting his equipment up, David came back over to her, with his hand on her waist, he told her, "That was really good."

"It was," Gina was grinning. Her client was happy, and so was she. And truthfully, being this close to David with his hand on her was doing a lot for her mood as well. Gina glance over at David's dad, he was tugging at his tie. "You might want to let your dad put on his pj's so he can get comfortable."

"Come on, Dad. Let me help you get into your pajamas." David removed his hand from her lower back and went to his father. As the two men went into the bathroom, Gina asked Mary, "Are you okay with how everything was handled today?"

"It was beautiful. I'm so glad you had that DVD with you. My husband was really with us today." Mary's hand went to her mouth as her voice broke. "I just don't know how to thank you."

Gina hugged the woman. "You don't have to thank me at all. I was happy to do it."

The bathroom door opened, and the men came back into the room. Mary wiped the tears from her eyes as Gina said, "It was so nice to meet you today, Mr. Pittman. I hope we didn't tire you out too much."

Senior lifted a hand and waved off her concerns. "It was my pleasure." As he got in his bed, he told Gina, "You can come back anytime you get ready."

"Thank you, sir." It made Gina feel good that her presence didn't bother the ailing man.

As David pulled the covers up to his father's chest, Senior said, "I'm proud of you, Son. You finally found the gold."

David's eyes widened as he turned to look at Gina.

Then his father asked, "When's the wedding?"

"Huh?" David turned back to his father, confusion etched in his face. He looked back at Gina and then told his father, "We haven't set a date yet."

"Don't make me and your mama wait too long. We'd like to see some grandkids while we're still kicking and breathing."

12

David and Gina stood by the door, talking with his mom as they readied to leave. But Senior was having none of that. "You not running off again, are you, Mary?"

Turning her head in her husband's directions, Mary said, "No, Dave, I'm not going anywhere." She then turned back to David, "I wish I had brought my nightgown, the nursing home lets me stay whenever he remembers me because he gets so upset when I leave. Everything was so rushed this morning that I didn't think to bring a change of clothes."

David told her, "There's a mall down the street. I can take you over there so you can pick out a gown and an outfit for tomorrow."

"Thanks for offering, but I don't want to leave your father and then get back here and he's forgotten me all over again."

"I can go for you," Gina offered. "You're what, a size seven?"

Grinning, Mary said, "I hide it well, dear, but I'm a ten. If you wouldn't mind picking me out something, I would greatly appreciate it. I'll even bake you a cake to take home with you. How's that?"

"Sounds lovely," Gina said, then she and David rushed out of the nursing home and headed down the street to the mall.

David put her hand in his as he parked the car. "I really want to thank you for today. My mom hasn't smiled so much since this madness began. She might just bake you two cakes tomorrow morning."

"That depends on if I get her the right gown to ensure she has a really good night."

David put his hands over his ears. "Hey, that's my parents you're talking about. I don't want to even think about that. And I definitely don't want to see the gown you pick out. So, please don't show it to me."

"Stop being silly, David. They are married, of course, they have sex."

"I'm not listening to you," He got out of the car and put his hands back over his ears again.

Laughing, Gina followed behind him, "How do you think you got here?"

"La-la-la-la."

"Now, you're going to sing and act like a two-year-old."

"Am not," David said while sticking his fingers in his ear and sticking his tongue out.

"Yeah, real mature." She pulled his fingers out of his ears. "You win. Your parents only shake hands and give forehead kisses."

"Thank you." He put an arm around her and they walked into the mall together. "The only kissing I want to talk about is the one you said happened when we were in college. Now, I know I had a drinking problem in all, but are you sure we kissed back then?"

"How did we get on this subject?"

He knew it was inappropriate. Gina was his publicist, and he signed her checks, but the woman intrigued him. She was mouthy and all about her business, but she was also a caring person and she loved her parents as much as he loved his own. She made him want to know more about her. And every time he looked at those lips of hers, he wanted to kiss her. So he said, "I just can't believe that I could have forgotten a kiss with you."

"Well, you did. But you were drunk and can't be held accountable for your actions, so I forgive you."

"Oh, you forgive me, huh." He stopped in the middle of the mall, turned her to face him. They were almost nose to nose when he asked, "Would you have to forgive me if I kissed you right now? Or would you be okay with it?"

He could feel the heat as it built between them. She was in to him just as much as he was in to her. But he wouldn't kiss her unless she said it was okay. *Please, God, let her say it's okay.*

"David Pittman!"

A woman behind him shouted his name like she was trying to make a scene. He recognized the voice and groaned as he turned away from Gina to face the enemy. "What do you want, Michelle?"

"Did you get my text?"

He didn't answer.

"You think I'm playing with you. And look at your trifflin' behind. Got me pregnant, and now you in this mall with some other chick." She turned her sights on Gina. "Has he hit you yet, because he will trust me, I know first hand."

"Stop lying, Michelle. I didn't get you pregnant and I didn't hit you." David felt a tension headache coming on. He should have prayed about getting involved with this woman. But he had this thing about beautiful women, and Michelle was all of that. Every time he looked at her, he thought of Kerry Washington. Oh yeah, she was all beauty on the outside, but her heart was dark and corroded.

Michelle pointed at her eye as she shouted for anyone to hear. "Look at my eye and tell me you didn't hit me." She turned this way and that as people began to gather around them. "You see what he did to me? Mr. Superstar David Pittman blacked my eye."

"That looks fresh," Gina said as she walked closer to the woman. "When did he hit you?"

"Yesterday, at my apartment," Michelle spat the words like fire.

"You're lying. David was with me all yesterday and today, and we have proof to back that up. Do you have any proof to back up the lies you're telling?" Gina kept advancing on the woman.

"I don't need proof. He did it." She pointed to her eye again. "Look what he did to me."

Examine her eye, Gina shook her head. "I feel sorry for you because someone has been beating on you, but it's not David."

"You don't know him like I do," Michelle told her.

"Did you go to the police?" Gina asked.

"This is none of your business." Michelle gave Gina the hand as she stepped to David. Pointing in his face and getting loud like he owed her rent money. "You gon' regret doing me like this. I'm not the kind of woman to just take no and then go on about my business. So you better pay up!"

"Why are you doing this, Michelle. You know I don't owe you anything. I didn't do anything to you," David tried to reason with the woman.

"You owe me everything," Michelle declared.

David's eyes flashed with confusion. "Are you off your meds or something?"

Michelle spat in his face and then slapped him.

"Girl, have you lost your mind." David was enraged, yet he didn't strike back. One of the onlookers handed him a tissue.

"Oh, that's it!" Gina took her cell phone out of her purse. While David whipped the spit from his face, she dialed 911. "I'm calling the police."

"Call them," Michelle said, hands on hips. "He's the one whose going to jail. I've got the black eye, remember?"

Ignoring the maniac in front of her, Gina reported the incident. Mall security was approaching as the woman tried to strike Gina. The security guard restrained her. "The police are on the way, Gina told him as she hung up the phone.

Once again, David was amazed at Gina. Because if she hadn't been with him, he'd probably be the one being carted off to jail instead of Michelle. But because she was such a loudmouth, David had thirty witnesses and they were only too happy to tell the police what they saw.

~~~

"What a day, what a day, what a day," Gina kept saying that to herself while in her hotel room, packing her bag to head home in the morning. She was just happy that David was finally able to purchase the items that his mother needed. They took them back to the nursing home and then she grabbed some take-out and drove straight to the hotel.

She was worn out and needed to get some rest. Putting her pajamas on, Gina climbed in bed and was about to let her head hit the pillow, but her cell phone rang. She picked it up off the nightstand and saw that Toya was calling. "Hey girl, you back from your two-week-long honeymoon?"

"And not a minute too soon, I see. Did you know that you are trending on Twitter?"

Sitting up straight in bed, Gina said, "What? Why would I be trending?" Then she realized that every one of those onlookers at the mall probably had their cell phone with them. So much for improving David's image. If his Foodie network TV deal was in jeopardy before, it was scrapped at this point. "Oh my God, I didn't even think about people that might be recording."

"Oh, they recorded it, alright. And if you're interested, you're trending as 'The Lie Slayer'."

"The Lie Slayer, huh?" Gina repeated after Toya as she grabbed her laptop bag and turned on the computer. "The woman was lying through her teeth. But what I can't figure out is why she is doing this to him."

"She looked like she was out of her mind. But she didn't scare you. My friend put the po-po on her."

Shaking her head as she waiting on her computer to load, Gina said, "I don't even want to talk about that woman right now. Tell me about the honeymoon and let me live vicariously through you and Jarrod."

"We loved every minute of it. When Jarrod first surprised me with two weeks away, I thought that was too much time, that we'd get bored and be longing for home. But that was not the case at all, girl. We did everything we could think of, couple massages, long walks, we ate at so many restaurants that I brought ten extra pounds back with me."

"You'll work that off at the gym, so don't give it a second thought."

"I'm headed to the gym first thing in the morning," Toya told her.

"Too bad, I won't be home until tomorrow afternoon or I'd go with you."

"So, you have to leave David, are you going to be okay? Do I need to come over and give you a shoulder to cry on?"

"What are you talking about, Toya. I am on an assignment. I'm working for David. There's nothing romantic going on, so I doubt I'll be crying." Gina was not about to tell Toya about the kiss that almost happened between her and David at the mall. David was just messing around with her. He had just gotten caught in the moment. Because she saw the type of women that attract David, and Gina doubted that she was his type.

"Well, you sure looked like you were defending your man. And he looked like he wanted to take a swing at that woman."

"Of course, he wanted to take a swing. She spit on him for goodness sake."

Toya told her. "I saw that. How nasty do you have to be to spit on someone? But David didn't look like he wanted to fight when she spit on him, or even after she slapped him. He looked more like he wanted to be anywhere but there, like he wanted to escape. But he was about to leap on that woman when she tried to hit you. I'm telling you, if that security guard hadn't been there, David and that woman would have been carted off to jail, because he would have hit her."

"So, what are you saying, Toya? Do you think David is violent? You think he could have hit Michelle? Because if he had done that, he would have validated everything she's been saying about him."

"I don't think you're hearing me, Gina." Toya tried to make it plain to her friend. "David is an ex-football player, which is a violent sport. But don't see him as a violent man. What I did see was something in his eyes when that woman tried to swing on you. And yes, I think he would have hit her, but only to protect you."

"David doesn't need to protect me," Gina said, and I certainly wouldn't want him to lay hands on any woman, not even that nutcase we just dealt with."

"Of course not," Toya agreed. "But I think the man is falling in love with you. I could see it in his eyes."

Gina laughed at that. "If you saw the beautiful women that this man has at his disposal, you'd know that David isn't thinking about me." But something in Gina rejoiced at Toya's words. Why did Toya's statement excite her? She knew the man's reputation with women. But didn't operate like that anymore, Gina was convinced of that, but she wasn't trying to hang around for the backslide.

"You need to watch that video, Ms. Lie Slayer."

"Will you be at church on Sunday?" Gina wanted to know.

"Yes, ma'am."

"Okay, let me get off this phone and check out this video. I'll see you on Sunday." As they hung up the phone, Gina's computer had finally loaded. She went to Twitter and typed in The Lie Slayer.

13

"Did you sleep well," David asked as she drove them to the airport.

"I should be asking you that, since you're the one who had the eventful evening. The whole incident is trending on Twitter."

"And Facebook and Instagram," he added. "Friends kept calling me all night, but I didn't even open the video. But you're right, I didn't get much sleep, because I spent a lot of time praying."

"You did, huh? Do you mind if I ask what you prayed about?" The look he gave told her the question embarrassed him. "I didn't mean to pry. You don't have to tell me."

"No, it's okay. I was praying about my decision making and the type of women I have allowed into my life. I want to learn how to judge a woman more for what's in her heart than her outer appearance."

Giggling, Gina asked, "So now you're going to start dating ugly women with good hearts?"

Holding up a hand to slow her roll, he said, "Let's not get stupid up in here. My daddy told you that I like the pretty ladies, but let's just say I'm not just looking for pretty anymore. I'm also looking for substance."

"Yeah, 'cause Michelle didn't have any substance... more like she might be a substance abuser."

"Right, that's what I'm thinking. That girl is on a little somin-somin." David shook his head. "She was willin' out. Straight buggin'."

"Does she live in Dallas?" Gina asked.

"Not that I'm aware of. I met her at a party in New York, and as far as I knew, that's where she lived. Why she was out here, I couldn't tell you."

"I hope she hasn't started stalking you."

"You and me, both. But I think the restraining order I'm going to file should stop that."

"Good, you should get that filed a-sap. Before she tries to file one on you now that her scheme is out in the open."

Gina parked the car in the rental car lot. Then David held on to her hand as he turned to her. "I wanted to thank you for believing me and not thinking badly of me just because Michelle started spouting off a bunch of lies."

"You don't have to thank me, I know she's lying on you, and if I am called as a witness, I would go to court and tell them exactly how I know she's a big liar and schemer."

"Yeah, but how can you be so sure you're right? Most women would have been giving me the side-eye and thinking I got what I deserved for blacking her eye. Which I didn't do," He made sure to get that out there.

"I'm not most women." Gina lowered her head and ran her hand across her forehead. When she looked back up at him, she said, "I'm going to share something with you that I don't talk about a lot. My parents don't even know much about this. But I had a black eye like Michelle. I also had a broken arm and bruised ribs."

David's eyes widened as he leaned back, looking at her as if seeing her for the first time.

"I was a victim of domestic violence, and I didn't run up on the man who abused me like Michelle ran up in your face." A tear trickled down her face, David wiped it away. "I was so terrified of that man that I did whatever he said, all the while plotting my escape.

"I had to quit a job I loved, and I was earning good money. I even left the country to get away from that man. If you had done everything Michelle claims you did to her, she wouldn't be running up on you and attacking you, she'd be trying to be invisible whenever you were around. Just hoping that she'd escape one more degrading moment of abuse."

"I don't know what to say... I'm so sorry that you went through something like that." His fist tightened as his nose flared. "I would have crushed that man with my bare hands had I known you at that time. It kills me to think about you being abused like that."

"That doesn't mean I need you to become an abuser in order to defend me, okay." Gina was very leery of anyone who thought violence solved problems. Marvel used to talk like that, then the next thing she knew, he was laying hands on her.

"You might not need me to do it, but I'm not just standing around with my hands in my pocket if someone tried to hurt you, believe that."

Gina was done talking about this. She got out of the car and took the keys to the rental office inside the airport. They then went to the terminal and waited for their flight.

"You're not talking to me now or what?" David asked.

"I'm checking on your social media pages. We were busy this week, and I want to know if your fans are engaging." She had her phone up to her face and didn't even look at him as she answered.

"You sitting over there looking all tight like it's all business between us now?" When she didn't respond, he asked, "Is that it?"

"I'm working, David. I'm not here to entertain you."

Lifting an eyebrow, he said, "Oh, it's like that. Well, let me give you some space." David got up and took a seat in the next row over.

Out the corner of her eye, she saw him walk away. She wanted to say something, or at least stop tripping because she really shouldn't be so upset over the fact that he wanted to protect her. But, last night Toya had said that it looked like David wanted to hit Michelle, and now he tells her that he would harm someone for her. Another woman might be flatter with that, but to her, it sounded more like warning signs. Stay away.

But while she was staying away, another woman waltzed over to him. She heard the woman ask, "Aren't you David Pittman?"

He nodded.

She giggled. "I used to watch you every Sunday. You had some skills."

"Thank you."

The woman looked at the seat next to him. "Are you by yourself? Because if you are, I can keep you company."

Gina wanted to gag. Yes, David was handsome, and yes, he was rich and talented, but did these women have to throw themselves at him like he was the only man left on God's green earth. She rolled her eyes as he looked back at her.

David turned away from Gina and told the woman. "I was with someone, but she didn't want to be bothered, so it looks like I'm all alone and lonely."

"That just won't do," the woman said as she sat down next to David, opened her purse and pulled out a business card. "Call me, I'll make sure you're never lonely again."

"Are you serious?" Gina butted into the conversation.

"Uh-uh, don't do that." David waved a hand at Gina. "You didn't want to be bothered with me, so don't throw salt now that you see someone else wants me."

"Someone else is always wanting you. That's your problem, you got a big head because these women keep throwing numbers at you."

"Excuse me?" The woman turned to Gina. "You don't know me, I appreciate you staying out of my business."

"It's not even about you. I'm standing up for women in general." She pointed toward David. "Ask this man how many business cards has he collected this week, and then you'll realize that he was just feeding you a line. He's not alone at all."

The woman stood up. She told David, "It looks like you're not alone after all. I'll leave you to her while I go check on my flight."

As she walked away, David turned back to Gina. "Just shaking my head," he said and did so.

Gina wanted to tell him to stop shaking his head. But she had the good grace to realize that she was wrong. She had no business butting into David's life. He could take as many business cards as he wanted, he could call all the women he wanted. "I'm sorry, David, I was way out of line. I don't know what happened right there."

He nodded. "I think we both got a little heated. Let's just get this trip over with and take care of business on The Grind and I'm good.

"Speaking of that," Gina got out of her seat and joined him in the next row. "I have another idea that I think will take your grind to the next level."

"I'm listening."

"Remember those pictures you have on the wall at your restaurant?"

He nodded again.

"I think we need to go back to your restaurant and do a few videos. I want you to stand next to some of the photos and talk about why you selected that person to be on your wall of trust. Then I want you to invite a few of them to be with you on The Grind. We'll get the cameraman on The Grind to pan the audience and show each of your guests as they roll the film on these people who have meant so much to you in every area of your business and life."

"That's perfect, Gina. I'll give some of them a call to see if they can make it." He smiled at her and nudged her shoulder. "See, we work good together."

14

Gina needed to get away from David, but they were now on a two and a half hour flight. She was seated next to him and his cologne was driving her crazy because it was pure sex appeal. Or maybe it was the man himself who exuded sex appeal. Wasn't that why these women were always throwing themselves at him?

And what was she thinking by getting in his business like that? That woman had every right to give David her business card, but the truth of the matter was that she was jealous. But why was she jealous and why did she act like that when there was nothing between her and David?

"What's on your mind?" David asked as he nudged her.

She jumped. "Who me?"

"No, I want to know what the pilot is thinking?"

Resting her head against the headrest, she told me, "You don't want to know what's on my mind. It's not like I'm thinking about world hunger or how to solve it. Actually, I wish I knew how to solve world hunger and a few other things."

Shifting his body so he was facing her, he said, "Why are you changing the subject? You must have been thinking about me and don't want to admit it."

"See what I mean. All those women chasing after you has given you the big head. My every waking moment isn't spent thinking about David Pittman."

"I didn't say it was, but you were thinking about me just now. Why can't you just admit it?"

He was staring at her with those warm brown eyes of his. Eyes that seem to read her like a book. "Okay, I was thinking about how terribly I treated that woman who shamelessly threw herself at you. I had no right to act like that."

"And you already apologized," he reminded her.

"I know. I just feel bad because I shouldn't have acted like that."

"You can make it up to me by giving up some of that cake my mother baked you this morning."

Gina stuck her lip out and shook her head. "But it's German chocolate. Do you know how long it's been since I had a German chocolate cake?"

"It's been a while for me too and my mom makes the best German chocolate cakes I've ever eaten. So, you owe me for chasing that very nice lady away. Who knows, she could have been wife material. Maybe God Himself sent her over to me, and you ran her off with your rudeness."

She rolled her eyes heavenward, but gave in. "Okay, okay, I've give you some of my cake."

"Thank you," he leaned back in his seat and started flipping through a magazine.

"Let me ask you something," Gina said, interrupting his solitude. "Do you know a photographer who could handle this last session with you?"

"Not one who could get there tomorrow. Why, you got something else to do?"

No, she didn't have anything else to do. He was her only client. But she didn't want to be around him, up close and personal anymore. Things were getting uncomfortable between them and she wanted some distance. But those hospital bills weren't going to pay themselves, so she had to do that job she'd been hired to do and find some kind of way to stop thinking of David in any other way, but as a client. If she could afford to hire a photographer and send him to Ann Arbor, she would, but she couldn't. "I'll be there." Church was tomorrow, now she had something else to pray for.

~~~

Sunday morning was live at Christ Life. The praise and worship team brought the fire as they sang I Give Myself Away by William McDowell, then they broke out with Every Praise by Hezekiah Walker, Gina lost it. God had been good to her. He had pulled her out of the depths of despair. She had been in the process of losing everything, then along came this account and she was able to regain her footing. No, she wasn't completely out of debt. And she hadn't received the first bill for her father's surgery yet, so she was crossing her fingers and praying for a miracle on that bill. But God had made a way for her thus far and Gina believed He would see her all the way through.

Lifting her hands, Gina gave all the praise to her God. She loved her God, and He loved her. If He never did another thing for her, Gina wanted Him to know that she was grateful for what He'd already done. "Thank You, Jesus! Thank You, Jesus! She bowed down and as tears cascaded down her face, she kept praising. Kept her hands lifted, singing 'Every Praise'.

When praise and worship finished, Pastor Yvonne stood behind the pulpit to bring the message, Gina was transfixed as she listened to every word from her pastor. She read from Matthew, chapter 7:

Judge not, that ye be not judged. For with what judgment ye judge, ye shall be judged: and with what measure ye mete, it shall be measured to you again.

And why behold thou the mote that is in thy brother's eye, but consider not the beam that is in thine own eye? Or how wilt thou say to thy brother, Let me pull out the mote out of thine eye; and, behold, a beam is in thine own eye?

Thou hypocrite, first cast out the beam out of thine own eye; and then shalt thou see clearly to cast out the mote out of thy brother's eye.

Pastor Yvonne closed the Bible and looked out at the congregation. "This isn't going to be a fun message today. This is more of a take-your-medicine kind of message. And your medicine is the Word of God.

"Listen to me, Saints, too many of us spend too much time minding other people's business. And why are we in other people's business, because we don't like the way life has turned out for us, so we get in another man or woman's business, so we can judge them and make ourselves feel better. Because at least we don't act like so-and-so."

Moving from behind the pulpit to the side of it. She put a hand on the top of the pulpit while looking out at the congregation. "But the word of God tells us to 'judge not, lest we be judge'. Do you know why you don't want to be judged... because none of us are innocent. All have sinned, and your sin is not considered a small sin while the next person's sin is some huge, big deal. No, sin is sin and if it wasn't for the blood that covers our sins, we would all have a lot to answer for."

That hit home for Gina. She hadn't lived a perfect life, but she was sure judging David and the way he once lived his life. The man had changed and she hadn't given him credit for that. She had to admit it, she was judgmental. And the really awful thing about that was that she couldn't stand judgmental Christians.

"Wouldn't we be better off praying for the imperfections we see in others, rather than turning our superior noses up at them? I'm serious, Saints, I have never understood how we can claim to love our brothers and sisters in Christ on one hand, but then deny them the love of God with the other hand. Don't you know that the same God who loves and forgives you daily, wants to be that kind of God to other people in need of mercy as well?"

The message was powerful. Gina couldn't get it off her mind and had even considered going down to the altar prayer when Toya and Jarrod rushed over to her. They had been seated in the front pew, while she was in the fourth pew from the front, so she hadn't been able to speak to them during service. "Don't you two look well-rested and like you've been getting in some sun while the rest of us mid-westerner froze our butts off."

"Don't even trip," Jarrod told her. "Because we know you spent some time in Dallas while we were gone. And Dallas isn't cold like the mid-west in the winter."

"Who is telling my business? Just let me know so I can set them straight?" Gina teased, Jarrod.

"I'm not trying to get anyone in trouble, but David does have a big mouth. But actually, he only told me because you told him to invite some of his friends to The Grind for that grand finale episode."

"That's right, you do have a sandwich named after you, and a compelling story for the reason you have that honor. So, I'm glad he invited you." Gina turned to Toya, "Will you be coming to New York with Jarrod?"

"Girl, you know I'm not going to miss an opportunity to dine at a New York restaurant. I can't wait."

Gina was giddy at the news. "I'm so excited. I'll have my best friend with me while I complete an assignment that is guaranteed to get me more clients."

"And you know if I can do anything to help while we're there, just let me know," Toya told her.

"Oh, I was already thinking of ways to put you to work. I wish you were a photographer, then I could send you to Ann Arbor to shoot some video and snap a few photos of David tomorrow."

"Since I'm a lawyer instead of a photographer, I won't be able to do it. I have been gone from my practice for two weeks, I've got to get back on my grind."

"I understand," Gina said. "I'm just being a baby about facing David again. But it's my job, and I'm going to see it through to the finish."

"Has David done something to upset you," Jarrod asked while his hand rested on Toya's lower back.

Gina quickly shook her head. "If anything, he should be upset with me. I really needed today's message, because I've been so judgmental toward David. I haven't given him a chance. I wasn't even paying attention to all the ways he kept displaying that he is now a new creation in Christ, but I kept hitting him over the head with his past."

"So why don't you just apologize and let that be that," Toya suggested.

Gina nodded. "You're right. I just need to get the courage to admit how wrong I've been."

"I'm surprised by this," Jarrod told her. "With the way you defended David on the video that's gone viral, I would have sworn that the two of you were getting along real good if you know what I mean?" Jarrod's voice deepened and his eyebrows went up and down as he said, 'if you know what I mean'.

Toya poked her husband in the side. "How dare you suggest that my friend has been getting it on with David."

"Your comment just proves that I'm not the only one whose been misjudging David. Because he is not in these streets chasing after women." It wasn't her place to tell anyone that David had decided to be celibate until he found his wife. That was his own personal business. But she wasn't going to let Jarrod or anyone else think David was still some kind of playa-playa.

"I know that," Jarrod told her. "But the two of you looked like there was something special between you. Like each of you would go to bat for the other."

Gina didn't respond to that.

Then Jarrod asked, "Hey, that reminds me. Will Bill be in New York also?"

"Bill, who?"

"Bill Hoffman from the Buffalo Bills. I saw him on that video, I have his jersey, so if he's going to be in New York, I'll bring it with me to get it signed."

"I'll check with David and let you know."

15

"You really can't be serious with this call, right now," David had just left church and he had been feeling good because his pastor brought the house down preaching like the rapture was upon us. David was thankful that he was a part of a fire and brimstone ministry, because the way he had lived his life before Christ had him feeling like everything goes and whatever felt good, was alright with him. But Pastor North reminded his congregation that the day of judgment was coming. And although no man could judge you, we all would one day have to give an account for what we did on earth to the almighty God.

He only wished that Michelle had been in the congregation at church today, then maybe she would have heard something that could stop her from being such a wacko.

"You know you can give me that money, David. You're rich. Two million is nothing to you."

"Can you please text all of this to me so I can have proof to show the police that you are trying to extort me." David was so through dealing with this mess.

"You want me to leave you alone, right? You never want to see me again, I get it. But if you want me out of your hair, you're going to have to pay up. I'm not going anywhere without that money." She started screaming, "Do you hear me, David. I don't care what I have to do to get it. I'm getting it!"

"Why did they let you out of jail?"

"Why would they keep me for hitting some man who's been abusing me for months?"

"I know you didn't tell the police some mess like that, Michelle? I did nothing but try to treat you with respect, and now you're harassing me. So, let me tell you how this is going to play out. I'm going to the police station and filing a police report on you for extortion and I'm also filing for a restraining order."

"No! Wait! Don't go to the police, David," she was pleading with him. "I need that money. Do you think I'd be doing this to you if I didn't need the money? People like you donate money all the time and don't think twice about it. Why can't you help me out?"

"Help you out! Is this a joke?"

"I'm not joking, David. I'm in town and I can come to your restaurant to get the money."

"Don't you dare come anywhere near my place of business."

Michelle was insistent. "If I don't get that money, something really bad is going to happen. If you cared anything about me at all, then help me out."

"Get off my phone. And don't come within three hundred feet of me." He hung up the phone and drove straight to the police station. He hadn't done the restraining order when he was in Dallas because he just didn't want to deal with all the men laughing at him for being this tough ex-football player, who was now claiming that a woman was beating on him. But enough was enough. Michelle had to be stopped and maybe a restraining order would convince her to stay away from him.

He was still shaking his head as he pulled up to the police station. He couldn't believe the woman had the audacity to ask him to help her out all while threatening him with this 'something bad is going to happen if I don't get the money' business.

He walked into the station and immediately wanted to turn around and walk out the door. The woman standing behind the intake desk was the best friend of the girl he dated in college. The relationship didn't end well, and it had all been David's fault. She looked up from her desk and immediately frowned. "What can I do for you?"

"I need to file a restraining order."

She all but rolled her eyes as she asked, "Who are you filing this order against?"

"Her name is Michelle Dayton."

The officer grabbed a note pad and pen, she bent her head, but her shoulders were shaking from laughter.

"Excuse me? I don't get what's so funny."

"I-I'm s-sorry." She could barely catch her breath from laughing. As she managed to compose herself, she turned her head toward the back of the station and yelled, "Can I get someone for a domestic?" She then stood up and leaned over her desk as she quietly told David, "I knew you'd get what was coming to you one day. I'm just glad I was here to see it."

"You know what, Brenda, I'm not the same guy you knew in college. I've changed and I'd really like to apologize to Serita for the way I treated her. Can you give her that message?"

An officer walked up to them. "I'll take him," he told Brenda.

She snarled, after giving David a disgusted look, "You can have him." As David walked past her, she said, "And you can tell her yourself. She's at Forest Hill Cemetery after letting another man put his hands on her."

<p style="text-align:center">~~~</p>

"Hey Daddy-o, how ya' be?" Gina decided to stop in and check on her dad before heading to Ann Arbor to do the video and photoshoot with David. She was amazed to see that her father was sitting up watching television and he was no longer using the oxygen tank.

"I feel like a new man, baby-girl. That's how I be."

She sat down on the sofa next to her father's chair. "I'm so glad you are feeling better. Mom told me, but I had no idea that you were off the oxygen tank."

"That didn't happen until yesterday. My home health nurse contacted the doctor and he said I could try it for a while without the oxygen. Your mom checks my oxygen levels a few times a day and I'm staying steady." He gave her the thumbs up.

Receiving this news from her dad made her sacrifice worth it all. She had started packing up her apartment and would be moving into her old room when she came back from New York. Gina hadn't lived at home since she left for college. But she could do this if it meant paying off her dad's hospital bills so that they could stay in the home they loved.

"So, I hear you're moving back home for a bit," her father said.

"Yep, I'm packing now."

"Well, you just remember that we have an eleven o'clock curfew around here. "He shook a finger at her as if she was a disobedient child.

Laughing at him, she said, "I'm going to need at least a midnight curfew, Dad. Let's compromise. I mean, I am thirty-five."

"We had this same conversation when you were sixteen, and what was my answer?"

"You said that 'ain't nothing open that late but liquor stores and legs'. But guess what, Dad... Walmart is now open that late and a few fast-food restaurants as well."

"Okay, you got me there." He smiled at his daughter. "No curfew this time."

Gina leaned over and hugged her father. "Thanks, Dad."

"No baby-girl, I need to thank you. If I'd listened when my mother begged me to stop smoking, I wouldn't be in this predicament and your mom wouldn't have to worry that we might have to sell the house to cover my hospital bills. I appreciate that you are willing to help your old man out like this."

"I must have been raised right, huh?"

Before her father could answer that, her mother came running into the room, shouting, "You won't believe this! I promise you won't believe this!" Audrey was so excited she started jumping around the room.

"Woman, will you spill it already? What has happened to get you this excited," her husband asked.

She bent down and kissed him. While still leaning over with hands on both armrests of his chair, she told him, "Even though I'm excited, I want you to remain calm. You are not allowed to jump out of your seat. You have to remain seated, okay?"

"Okay, I promise."

Audrey straightened back up, she looked from Gina and then back at her husband. Taking a deep breath to calm herself, she told them. "On Friday, we received the final bill for your surgery. I didn't tell you about it because it looked like they overcharged us a couple thousand. I planned to call them this morning to complain."

"Why didn't you tell me if there was a problem with the bill, Audrey. I don't like you hiding things like that from me." George shook his head.

"How much was the bill, Mom?" Gina was getting nervous. If the hospital was going to overcharge, it would take her longer to pay off the bill, which meant that she would be living with her parents longer than she expected.

"The bill was twenty-five thousand after Medicare paid their share." Both Gina and George groaned.

"But, as of this morning, we owe zero on the bill... nothing, nada. It's been paid and we are debt-free again." Audrey did a quick dance. "My God is an awesome God!"

Gina jumped out of her seat. "What!? Are you saying the bill has been paid or the hospital made a clerical error?" The distinction was important because if the hospital made an error, they would soon fix it and they would still owe all of that money.

"No mistake, hon. The clerk I spoke with told me that someone called their office this morning and paid the bill." Audrey was grinning from ear to ear.

"Who would do that?" George wanted to know.

"Who cares," Audrey told him. "It was an anonymous payment, but the clerk said it happens every now and then. People normally pay other people's bills at the end of the year so they can claim it on their taxes. She said it rarely happens at the beginning of the year, but I don't care. I'm looking at this as a gift from God." Audrey plopped down in her chair, looking a thousand pounds lighter.

"You've been really worried about that bill, haven't you, Mom?"

"I hated the idea of selling the house, but I also hated the thought of taking your money to pay our bills when I know you're struggling yourself."

"I'm not struggling, Mom. Things are fine." Gina didn't want her parents worrying about her.

Her mom wasn't letting her get away with that statement. "If things are so fine, why do you have a 'For Sale' sign on your car? Why are you moving back in with us?'

"I admit that I wouldn't be able to afford to pay my bills and the hospital bill, so I just decided to do a reset. But I'm okay, Mom. I really am."

"Now you are," her dad said. "Now that you don't have to worry about paying off your parent's debts." Tears welled up in George's eyes.

"I wonder who paid off the bill?" Audrey said with eyes full of joy.

Wiping the tears from his eyes as George said, "Y'all know that I've always paid my own way. I worked three jobs and your mom worked two, so we could put you through college. And you finished with no debt. I'm proud of that. But after we retired and I got sick, money just wasn't as easy to come by. It hurt my heart that you had to give up everything to help us. But to tell you the truth, I knew we needed the help."

He squeezed his wife's hand. "Because if I didn't take the help, I'd have to sell this house and take your mom away from the home we built together. So, I don't even care who paid that bill. I don't want to know. I just want to thank the Lord for His goodness and that's that."

Gina's father may not want to know who paid the bill, but she still wanted to know. And she thought she had an idea who anonymous was, and she was on her way to see him.

16

The End Zone was closed on Mondays, but Gina was surprised that the door was locked because she and David had an appointment set for noon. Gina glanced at her watch. It was 11:59 am. She went back to her car. Turned on the engine so she could warm the car back up and waited.

Fifteen minutes later, she picked up her cell and called David. He answered on the third ring. He sounded groggy. "Were you sleep? Did you forget we had an appointment today?"

"Ah, wow, what time is it?"

"Twelve-fifteen." Irritation was etched in her voice, but she couldn't help it. Her time was just as valuable as his.

"I'm getting up. I was laying down in my office and fell asleep. I'll unlock the door now."

She hung up the phone, turned her car back off and got out of the car. He opened the door and she went inside. "I didn't see your car outside, so I thought you just weren't here yet. If I would have known you were in here, I would have beat on the door or something."

He closed the door behind her. She then turned around to face him. David was disheveled and unkempt, like he had slept in the same clothes for the past three days, hadn't brushed his hair or washed his face. But she'd just seen him two days ago, so Gina didn't understand what could've happened to him in such a short time. "Are you okay," she asked concern written all over her face.

"I'm good. Let's get to work." He tried to walk past her, but she grabbed his arm and brought him full stop in front of her.

"I know that I'm just an employee and all, but I've gotten to know you in this last month that we've been working together. But you are normally upbeat and always on point with gear." She pointed at his wrinkled clothes. "You look like you fell out of a laundry bin. And don't get me started on that hair."

He touched his head.

Gina said, "and that face. When's the last time you shaved? How am I supposed to get good pictures with you looking like this?"

Touching his face, David said, "Wow, you really know how to make a man feel better. I'll go shave, goodness."

"Yes, I want you to shave, but first I want to talk to you. Can we sit over here for a minute." She directed him over to a table in the back of the restaurant. When they were seated, she told him. "I actually thought you'd be in a good mood when I saw you today because of the good deed you did for my family."

His eyes flashed up at her. "What are you talking about?"

"Good try, but your eyes gave it away. You know exactly what I'm talking about. And I want to thank you and let you know that I plan to pay every cent back to you."

He shook his head. "You don't owe me anything. I was paying off a debt that I owe."

Gina was confused. "But you don't owe me anything."

"Just let it go, Gina. I'm paying it forward, okay."

"No, it's not okay. You can't just pay my father's hospital bill, which was over twenty thousand dollars and not explain yourself."

David put his head in his hand and massaged his forehead. "Why you so difficult?"

"I'm not difficult. Why are you so moody and what does my father's hospital bill have to do with it?"

"Okay, here it is." He stretched out his arms as if ready to bare his soul. "You were right about me. I'm no good, I'm arrogant and I use and abuse people."

"What? Where is all this coming from? Are you still mad about me telling that woman about how many women give you their business cards? 'Cause I've already apologized for that. I was out of line." Gina was thankful for the message at church yesterday because she now understood that it wasn't right to judge David. He was a child with flaws just as she was. Her job was to encourage him to continue growing closer to the Lord.

"I don't care what you tell other women about me, Gina. Anything you say wouldn't even be half of how terrible I really am."

A car drove into the parking lot. Gina glanced out the window, wondering if someone was trying to get lunch and didn't realize that the End Zone was closed on Mondays. "Can we go to your office. I don't want anyone looking through the windows and seeing you like this."

"Again, with the insults." He just shook his head at her.

"I'm not insulting you." She stood up and looped her hand around his arm as she pulled him out of his seat. "I am your public relations coordinator and I'm not about to let you be seen like this."

They headed back to his office and then sat down on the sofa together. Gina gave him a moment and then said, "Talk to me, David. I don't have a picture on your wall of trust, but I promise I'm not going to tell your business."

He let out a self-deprecating laugh that fell flat. "I didn't mean to invite you to my pity party. But I've got to be honest, I got hit hard yesterday. And it's only because of Christ in my life that I called the hospital to pay your father's bill instead of driving to the liquor store to ease my pain. So, just give me a few minutes to get myself together and we can get to work."

"But why did you do it? What happened to you? Did it have anything to do with Michelle?"

David slumped in his seat and leaned his head against the back of the sofa. "Yes, it started with Michelle. She called me as I was driving home from church yesterday. She basically threatened me saying that if I didn't give her the money that something bad was going to happen."

"What was she talking about?"

"I don't know. She wouldn't explain. Just said that something bad was going to happen. I figured she was trying to threaten me again so I drove straight to the police station to file a report against her."

Gina clapped her hands. "I'm so glad you finally did that. Michelle needs to be stopped before she goes too far."

But David didn't seem pleased with himself. He looked sick. He closed his eyes, real tight like he was trying to block out something. "Brenda was there."

"Who is Brenda?" Gina let out a loud huff. "Don't tell me another chick gave you her number?"

"Nothing like that. Brenda was best friends with my ex-girlfriend from college. Her name was Serita Holmes."

Gina snapped her fingers. "I remember them. I had a couple of classes with Brenda. She was studying criminal justice or something like that."

"Must have been since she became a cop," David said.

"I didn't know Serita all that well. She was a cheerleader, wasn't she?"

"Yep," David nodded. "She was always so cheerful and just a downright good person. She never should have dated me, at least not back then when I was just a teenage boy listening to everybody tell me how great I was."

"You did have the big-head syndrome back then." David gave Gina a look that said, I-don't-need-your-help-with-this. She lifted a hand in surrender. "Sorry, please finish your story."

"Anyway, I wasn't a good guy for Serita. As you know, I was going around campus kissing on every available girl I could find. Serita kept putting up with me, then one day I caught her out with this guy. I strong-armed her back to my dorm room and started pushing her around. I was so embarrassed that she could do me like that... I wanted to punch her. But she started crying.

"You see, I had been squeezing her arm so tight and shaking her that it caused a bruise on her arm. When Brenda saw her arm, she tried to get Serita to go to the police and file a report on me. But my coach talked her out of it. Because the incident happened the week before the big game and nobody wanted bad press for the school or its star athlete."

"I'm not gon' lie, I was happy that my coach dealt with the situation because my mama and grandmother would have beat me down if they knew about that incident. And it could have meant the end of my football career."

Gina didn't know what to say. David had abused a girl back in college, and they basically covered it up. "Did you and Serita keep seeing each other after that?"

"We did, but to be honest with you, a part of me lost respect for her for staying with me. Deep inside, I knew that I was wrong. I never laid a hand on her or any other woman after that night because I felt so guilty. I've done many things wrong in my life, but I never wanted to be that type of man. And having Serita around reminded me of the type of man I could be if I lose control. So, I dumped her right before I got drafted."

"Nice guy," Gina said as she tsk-tsked-tsked with her hands.

"I'm not perfect. But if I could take it back, I would a thousand times. Because I found out from Brenda that Serita is dead. Some guy she was seeing beat her to death."

"Oh, my God." Gina put her hand to her chest. "I'm so sorry to hear that."

"I had no idea either, but apparently, Brenda thinks it's my fault, and maybe it is. Because I was Serita's first serious boyfriend and if she judged relationships, by the way, I treated her, maybe she didn't realize she deserved better."

"Wait, what?" Gina got on her knees on the sofa, put her hands on David's shoulders and forced him to look up at her. "Are you telling me that because of a foolish mistake you made at nineteen, that Serita's death is your fault all these years later, even though it was some other man who killed her?"

"Maybe she wouldn't have picked a guy like that if she hadn't been with a guy like me in the first place."

"Or maybe, just maybe when you asked God to forgive you for your sins and you gave Him your life, He actually did forgive you and is not holding you responsible for what someone else did."

"Brenda says that what Michelle is doing to me is justice for what I did to Serita."

131

Where did all these judge and jury type people come from? Did any of them have a pastor like Pastor Yvonne, who was willing to stand in the pulpit and tell them that they had no right to judge others? All judgment belonged to God. "Have you considered the fact that Brenda might be going through something that might cause her to still be holding this in her heart against you after all these years?"

"You held that kiss against me. And I promise you I was young and stupid back then, but that hasn't stopped anyone from feeling some type of way about me."

She sat back down on the sofa. Okay, he was right. She had felt humiliated back in college when David had kissed her one night and then acted like he didn't even know her the next day. And yeah, she had judged him and his behavior without taking into account God's ability to redeem and to change any man or woman who wants to be changed. "Do you have a Bible here?"

He walked over to his desk, opened the top drawer, and pulled out his Bible. "I've been studying whenever I have time." He sat back on the sofa and handed it to Gina.

"I want you to study Matthew, Chapter seven. Start by reading verses 1-6." She opened the Bible and turned to the book of Matthew. "My pastor preached on this yesterday and it made everything so clear to me."

After spending a few minutes reading the scriptures, David turned back to Gina and said, "So basically, all the people who constantly judge me for my past behavior, are hypocrites because they have probably done just as much if not more than anything I've done."

"Even more than that. Because if God has judged you and found you worthy of forgiveness, then don't you think you should also forgive yourself?"

"Wow, now that's deep, I hadn't looked at it that way." David turned back to the Bible and began reading out loud from verses 7-11. "Check this out."

"Ask, and it shall be given you; seek, and ye shall find; knock, and it shall be opened unto you: For every one that asks receives; and he that seeks finds; and to him that knocks it shall be opened. Or what man is there of you, whom if his son ask bread, will he give him a stone?

Or if he ask a fish, will he give him a serpent? If ye then, being evil, know how to give good gifts unto your children, how much more shall your Father which is in heaven give good things to them that ask him?

After reading, he looked back at Gina and said, "Those scriptures describe your situation. Because I know you've been knocking on God's door, praying and pleading for God to come through for you. You put your car up for sale and you're even getting ready to move in with your parents just so you could help them out. God has sent you the blessing you've been seeking, so just accept it."

She had been praying and asking God to make a way out of no way for her, so why couldn't she just accept David's gift and move on. "But I don't understand. You said that paying off my father's hospital bills was your way of paying it forward. What exactly do you mean by that?"

He closed the Bible and looked at her for a long moment. Sighing, he said, "You're not going to let this go, are you?"

"If I paid off some huge bill for your parents, you'd want to know why."

"If I tell you, then you've got to drop this foolish notion of paying me back."

Gina shook her head. "No, that's not fair."

"Look at me, Gina. I may look a little rough around the edges today, but I'm not hurting for money. I didn't have to put a car up for sale or move in with my parents to pay that bill. And I promise you, I won't even miss that money. So, let me do this for you."

Was it pride that wouldn't let her accept this generous gift from David. She appreciated the help. But why? Does he view her as a charity case? "Tell me why and let's go from there, okay?"

"You are one stubborn woman. Okay, here it is. First of all, I have enjoyed spending time with you. The way you treated my parents did something to me; it made me realize that I care for you like I haven't cared about a woman in a long time. So, when I was feeling really low about what happened to Serita and wishing I could have done something for her, I thought about how you told me about the man who abused you and caused you to lose so much. I figured, if I couldn't help my ex, then I would help the woman I am praying will soon become a part of my future."

"Your future?" Gina couldn't believe what she was hearing. Did David truly care about her? Silly question, what man would plunk down thirty-thousand for a woman's family member if he didn't care anything about her? How did she feel about that?

He didn't give her much time to think about it before he leaned so close to her that she could smell the day-old scent of his cologne... still smelled good. He pressed his lips against hers, his lips were soft and warm against her. The kiss was soft and endearing at first. Then he pulled her close, held her tight as he got greedy and devoured her lips as if he'd been on a three day fast and she was the first meal in sight.

She panted and gasped for air when he finally let her go. Her mind was playing tricks on her because she'd never experienced a kiss so sensual, yet so endearing that she never wanted it to end. But now that it had, she didn't know what to do or what to say.

As David regained his ability to speak, he told her, "I can guarantee you that I'll never forget this kiss. Bible study and a kiss with the woman of my dreams, I'm a blessed man."

17

After the first kiss, David went into the bathroom and cleaned himself up. Thankfully, he kept extra clothes at the restaurant. He shaved and brushed his hair. He looked more like himself when he re-entered his office. "Better?"

"Much," Gina acknowledged. She took her camera out of its case. "Now, let gets some work done."

"If you want me to go inside the restaurant and do the videos, it's going to cost you another kiss," he told her as he stood in the doorway, blocking her exit.

"Come on, David, you don't need my lipstick on your lips while we're taking photos." She stood up and walked to the door, trying to get around him.

But David wasn't having it. He lowered his head and stole another kiss. This one was quick, but he could have sworn the earth moved as their lips parted. "Did you feel that?"

"What?" She asked as she stumbled. He caught her, and she was back in his arms again, he was coming in for another kiss. "Oh no, you don't, we have work to do."

"Is this last bit really needed. We've done so much work for this show. I can't see how one more thing is going to change anything."

"Are you kidding?" She walked over to his wall of trust with him. She made a sweeping motion with her arms. "These pictures are a part of your grind. These people have helped to move you forward in life and business in some shape or form. Having some of them in the audience while video of you explaining how they ended up on your wall of trust is pure gold."

"You're the expert, so I'll take direction from you on this."

"Good." She pointed at the picture of his grandmother. "Now, stand there."

"Oh, I can talk about Nana all day long." He smiled as he viewed the picture of the woman who had given him the skills that he now used in his second career.

One by one, she had him stand next to each picture and discuss why the person was so influential in his life and why he held them in such high esteem that he would create a wall of trust for them.

When David stood next to Bill Hoffman's picture and began saying, "Let me tell you about this man right here. I don't care what or where but if I'm in any kind of fight, I'm calling this guy right here. And you know what, I don't have a doubt that he'll come through for me."

While David was saying those words, Gina flashed back to something Jarrod had said at church the day before. "Hold on, I need to check on something."

"What's wrong?" He asked as he viewed the scowl on her face.

"I don't know. Does Bill live in Dallas?" She asked as she pulled her laptop out of the bag and turned it on.

"No, ma'am. He can't stand the heat. He lives in New York."

Her computer powered up, she went to Twitter and once again viewed the video of Michelle attacking David at the mall.

"Are you for real right now? Do you really think I want to watch that?" He tried to turn off her computer.

Gina snatched it away from him. "This is important, David. Let me watch this." She kept watching the video, searching the faces of the bystanders who stood around enjoying the show.

"How long is this going to take?"

"Shhh, I'm concentrating."

"Concentrating on what? I don't know what you expect to see other than I woman who is clearly off her meds."

She ignored him and kept watching. Then, as she watched the police put handcuffs on Michelle, she saw the woman struggle with the police and curse them out, jerking and screaming that David was the one who needed to be arrested. Then her eyes got real big and she looked terrified. She then stopped struggling against the police and walked out, submitted to the process. But it was at that moment that her eyes filled with terror that Gina saw the same man Jarrod must have seen when he watched the video. She hadn't noticed him before, because she had assumed that the thought of going to jail was the thing that terrified Michelle.

She stopped the video and rewind it. When she had it back at the spot she needed David to see she said, "Come over here and tell me if this is your friend Bill?"

David had a questioning look on his face. "What would Bill be doing in Dallas?" But he looked anyway, and then said, "Yeah, that's Bill."

"Do you notice how scared Michelle looks when she sees him?"

He sat down at the table with Gina, seeing things he didn't understand. "She does seem scared, doesn't she."

"Tell me something, David. How did you meet Michelle?"

He thought for a minute, then said, "It was at Bill's retirement party two years ago. But we didn't start dating until a year later, I ran into her again at a fundraising event. I was one of the speakers."

"And she told you that if she doesn't get that money, something bad is going to happen, right?"

"Right."

"Why don't you call and ask her to meet us at the restaurant. Tell her you're thinking about giving her the money."

"If I didn't know better, I'd think you were asking me to let a woman who I just filed a restraining order on back in my personal space."

"I know this isn't going to be easy for you, but you know how you said you wanted to help me because I had been abused." He nodded. "Well, the same thing goes for Michelle. She is being abused, and you can help her."

"I didn't abuse that woman," he shouted those words.

She put a hand over his to calm him. "I know you didn't. Remember, I'm the one who has believed you from the beginning."

"Not the beginning, you were going to quit because you thought I was a woman beater."

"Okay, well, I believed you once you explained everything to me." She rolled her eyes. "Is that truthful enough for you?"

"Yep, that's about right."

"Are you going to call her or not?"

"She spit in my face, Gina. Did you forget about that?" David shook his head. "I don't want to be anywhere near that woman for the rest of my life."

"Think about this for a minute, David. You tried to make atonement for your sin against Serita by paying a bill for me, but what if God put Michelle in your life for that very reason. I see this

139

so clearly now. Don't miss it, David. God has given you an assignment, will you help this woman or not?"

~~~

Michelle stepped inside the End Zone like it was Friday, and she was about to get paid. David escorted her to a table in the middle of the restaurant but when she saw Gina seated at the table, she bulked. "What's she doing here?"

"Gina is with me," he told her. "If you want this meeting, then you will have to talk to both of us, or you can leave right now." He shrugged. "Don't make me that much difference, Gina is the one who thinks we should help you."

"What? Gina tells you what to do with your money now? Mmph, I guess we didn't get that far in our relationship." She sat down and did the gooseneck while giving Gina the evil eye.

"Let's don't get it twisted and misrepresent up in here. You and I never had a relationship. I just took you out on a few dates. That's it."

The look on David's face told Gina everything she needed to know. He was ticked and would probably blow up in here if this meeting went left. So, she was going to try her best to keep everything on track. "Do you think we should eat now," Gina asked David, trying to give him something else to think about.

"Oh, yes, right." He turned back to Michelle. "I took the liberty of cooking a meal, so we can have something to chew on during our discussion. Let me bring the food in here." He left the two women alone as he went into the kitchen.

"I didn't ask for anything to eat," Michelle was aggravated. "And what do we need to talk about. I thought he was going to help me."

"We do want to help you, Michelle. But the help you need is not the money you are seeking."

"What do you know about it?" Michelle snapped at her.

Gina wasn't put off, she understood where the brass, hard exterior was coming from. "Actually, I know a lot about it. I've been where you are."

Michelle hissed, "You don't know anything about me. You're just David's new shiny object. But believe me, he'll get tired of you soon enough. And when he throws you away, you'll be trying to get paid just like I am, so don't sit there like you're so above me."

"I'm glad that your eye is healing. You can barely make out the bruise anymore."

Michelle lifted her hand and touched the space just below her left eye. "If David knew how to keep his hands to himself, I wouldn't've had a black eye in the first place."

"David didn't hit you, we both know you're lying about that. So, why don't we cut the charades so we can get somewhere."

"What are you talking about? You weren't there... you can't really say for sure whether he hit me or not."

Shaking her head, Gina declared, "I'm a hundred percent sure. And you know who else knew it also... the police."

Michelle opened her mouth to say something, then closed it and folded her arms around her chest in defiance. "Then why is David about to give me this money? I'll tell you because he's guilty. You just better beware and get away from him while you can. David is a vicious and angry man. He's unpredictable."

"That's the worst part about it, isn't it, the unpredictability. One day things will be going along great. He takes you out to dinner, he buys you flowers and tells you he loves you. The next day he's in a rage and you are nothing but a burden to him. Anything you say might set him off, so you keep quiet, but he hits you anyway."

"Yeah, that's how it was," Michelle agreed.

"I was terrified of the man who used to beat me. He told me that if I left him, he would find me and kill me. So I stayed even after he broke my arm and my ribs. I believed he would kill me. But I wanted out even more than I wanted to breathe, so I plotted my escape. I moved out of the country so he couldn't find me. That's how bad things had gotten for me."

Some of Michelle's defenses were falling as she stared at Gina as if she'd found a kindred spirit. "So you do know how it is?"

Gina nodded. "But I also know that you're not afraid of David, not even a little bit."

When she didn't respond, Gina said, "Can I show you something?"

Michelle looked around the room, which was empty except for her and Gina. "How much longer is David going to be?"

As if on cue, David came out of the kitchen pushing a cart towards them. "All the starving people in the house, raise your hand. I've got pasta with chicken or shrimp, salad and some garlic bread for us to feast on."

Gina raised both her hands. "You know I'm starving. I've been here all day, and you didn't feed me."

"I know you're not complaining because I'm always feeding you." He smiled at Gina with eyes that said, you-light-up-my-world.

She was grinning right back at him, oblivious to the fact that they had company.

Michelle harrumphed. "You too can stare at each other all day long for all I care." She stuck her hand out. "Can you just give me the money so I can be on my way."

David asked Gina, "Did you show her the video yet?"

"I was just getting to that when you came back in." Can we get our plates and then show the video?" Gina looked back to Michelle, do you mind hanging out with us for a few more minutes. I'm a witness that this man is an awesome chef. So you will enjoy the food."

Michelle harrumphed again. "He might be trying to poison me for all I know."

"Trust me, Michelle, I am not going to prison behind you and no one else," David assured her.

Gina got out of her chair. "I'll get my plate first. That way, if I don't croak, you'll know it's all good." Gina and David fixed their plates. David said grace and then they went for it, smacking their lips at each scrumptious bite.

"Okay, I'll eat." Michelle filled her plate and then joined them back at the table. "You never cooked for me while we dated, so I'm sure this was done just to impress Gina," she complained.

David squeezed Gina's hand as he looked into her eyes. "I like cooking for Gina. She appreciates good food, and that puts a smile on my face."

"Is this an act? Are you two trying to throw your love for each other in my face to make me feel some type of way because if it is, it's wasted on me. I simply don't care." Michelle put a fork full of pasta in her mouth and savored the taste.

Gina believed her. Michelle didn't care about David, his love life, or anything else that had to do with him. But Gina knew what the woman did care about. She put her laptop on the table as they ate and turned it back on. She had already downloaded the video and had it at the exact spot she needed.

As the video played, Michelle put her fork down. Her eyes widened as they came to the part where fear was clearly displayed in her eyes. Gina hit the pause button. "The look you have on your face right now is the same look you had when you saw Bill. He's the one you're afraid of, isn't he?"

"Bill, who? What are you talking about?" Michelle's hand shook as she tried to regain her composure.

"You were at Bill's party the night I met you, so please don't try to act like you don't know who he is." David pointed toward the laptop screen. "The look on your face when you saw him tells us you know exactly who you're looking at."

Michelle's shoulders slumped. "I never wanted to do this. But if I don't get that money from you today, something bad is going to happen."

David had told her that when Michelle said those words to him, he took it as a threat. But Gina wasn't so sure if Michelle had been threatening him at all. "Who is something bad going to happen to?" She asked Michelle.

Lowering her head as tears began to fall, Michelle said, "He's said he would kill me this time. I'm sorry David, I didn't want any parts of this, but Bill wants that money, and he will kill me if I don't get it."

"My abuser used to threaten me like that too," Gina told her. "But a kind elderly woman prayed for me, and suddenly I knew what I needed to do in order to get away from him. Can I pray for you, Michelle?"

18

The day had come, David and two other contestants were back on The Grind to determine a grand finale winner. But before a winner would be selected, the audience and the judges would view video clips on each of the contestant's restaurants to determine if they were handling their grind. They would also see video clips concerning the charity each contestant represented and the final event would be a cook-off. Actually, while the video clips are shown throughout the hour-long program, each of the contestants will be preparing their three-course meal.

"You ready for this?" Gina asked David."

He pulled her into an embrace and kissed her soundly. "I'm ready for anything as long as you are with me. Will you be with me, Gina?"

"I'm going to be right in the audience rooting for you all the way."

"I'm not just talking about today. I want you with me for a long, long time to come. You're the one I want, Gina."

The door to his dressing room opened and in walked his business manager. David smile, while still holding Gina close, he said, "Hey Katie, my lady, long time no see."

"I wouldn't go calling a woman your lady while you're holding onto another woman," Katie told him, then popped his arm with the manila folder she was holding.

"You mean this beautiful lady right here?" David pulled Gina closer and kissed the back of her neck. "I'm over the moon about her, Katie. Can't you tell?"

Katie smiled at him, "I can indeed. But I came in here to tell both of you that the network likes all the coverage they been seeing. And as long as everything goes well today, we should be in."

"That's awesome!" Gina exclaimed.

But David wasn't ready to jump for joy just yet. He told Katie, "I can't make any promises about how today will go. But I can tell you that I plan to be authentically me, and I'll just trust God with the rest. If it's His will for me to have this cooking show, then it will be. But I have to finish what I started."

Katie turned to Gina. "What's he talking about?"

Gina wiggled out of David's embrace. She told Katie, "Come on, let's take our seats because I guarantee that you don't want to miss a minute of this show."

Katie took the end seat on the front row. Gina sat in-between Mary and Toya. Jarrod was on the other side of Toya, and Bill sat next to Jarrod.

Mary leaned toward Gina. "Senior wasn't in any condition to fly this morning. I didn't want to upset him, so I let him stay at the home."

Gina saw the pain in the woman's face. She had no idea how hard it must be to love a man who didn't even recognize you most of the time. She hoped her news would bring some small comfort to Mary. "I have a surprise for you. I pitched the Alzheimer's story to NBC and Lester Holt wants to interview you."

"Me?" Mary looked surprised.

"Yes, Mary. They loved how you championed this issue at the Alzheimer's walk and how loving you are to your husband."

"Will Junior be able to fit this interview in his schedule?" She asked.

Gina shook her head. "He doesn't have to fit it in. Lester won't be interviewing David, just you. The angle for this story is about the power women display when faced with insurmountable odds. And they already have the film with you, David and your husband so they may use some clips from that."

Mary patted Gina's hand. "Thank you," she said with a shaky voice.

"It was my pleasure," Gina told her. The show began, so everyone was transfixed by the three contestants preparing their meals. The announcer spoke with each contestant as they prepared their meals.

When he reached David, the announcer said, "Now, as I understand it, all of the meals you are preparing have been named after people who are special to you."

David flashed that million-dollar smile toward the camera as he moved around the kitchen. "That's correct. Today, I'm preparing Beloved's Down Home Gumbo which is one of my father's favorites and is based on a creation out of his home town of New Orleans. I also have Jarrod's Crabby Cakes and for dessert, I will be serving Big Mama's Famous Sweet Potato Cheese Cake."

The announcer licked his lips. "Is that sweet potato cheesecake anything like them Patty pies?"

"What you talking 'bout? Patty ain't got nothing on my Big Mama."

Do it, baby! Gina wanted to shout and jump out of her seat; David was killing it. But she kept her composer and just relaxed in her seat. The contestants finished their meal and then stood before the judges. This was the part that kept Gina awake all night. How would the world receive David after this segment? She prayed that they would hear his heart and understand why he needed to do this on national television.

Just before the judges tasted the creations of one of the contestants, a two-minute video played. This video showed the contestant in the work environment to show off their grind and then it gave them time to highlight the charity they represented. Each contestant had a very good story to tell. However, David's video and food tasting were last because his was the most impactful and literally show-stopping.

As David came on the big screen for everyone in the audience to view, Gina held her breath. Pictures of him as a star athlete filled the screen; then within a flash, he was shown with an apron on and working in his restaurants. Then David was shown standing next to a picture of his father, who was on his wall of trust. "When I first began this competition, I picked Alzheimer's as the charity I wanted to donate to. I did that because my father has been dealing with this illness for the last five years and it has been really hard on my family." He held up a check that had an amount of fifty-thousand dollars on it. "To help other families suffering through this devastating illness, I am donating $25,000 to the Alzheimer foundation."

He walked away from his father's picture and then stood next to Bill Hoffman's picture. "I have decided to bring awareness to another devastating issue that millions of women deal with daily... domestic violence."

David looked straight into the camera as if searching for someone specific, then he said, "Mom, please forgive me, but when I was nineteen years old, I hit my girlfriend. Back then, I felt awful and vowed to never put my hands on another woman, and I have from that day to this. But Serita," David sighed as he looked very much ashamed of the man he used to be. "That was my college sweetheart's name. Anyway, Serita ran into another man who didn't just put his hands on her, he killed her. And I don't want that to happen to not another woman, so I want to help in any way I can. And if we can rescue just one woman from a violent situation, then we stop the pain that a family feels when they have to say goodbye too soon. So, I ask that we begin by helping Michelle."

As David said Michelle's name, the video clip cut from him to a woman seated in a chair facing the camera. She looked defeated and afraid but determined to do what was right. "My name is Michelle Dayton…

As Michelle told the story of how Bill Hoffman beat her when he discovered she was pregnant because he didn't want to pay child support to another woman, Bill squirmed and looked for the exit. However, there was a police officer stationed at each exit. When the show was over, and David was given the grinder trophy, the police headed toward Bill.

Bill jumped out of his seat and tried to run, but Jarrod tripped him. David made his way over to Bill just as the officers were handcuffing him.

"Just tell me why, Bill? We were supposed to be tight. How could you do something like that and then try to extort me for money?"

"You had it," Bill snarled. "You knew that the NFL had revoked my signing bonus after I retired; you knew that I had more child support than I could afford, but you didn't offer to help me with nothing."

"I didn't help you make them babies, why should I pay for them." David shook his head. "Whatever, man."

As the police carted Bill off, Katie walked over to David, holding out the cell phone to him. "It's for you. I can't believe it."

"Who is it?" He asked her.

"It's the CEO of the Foodie network. He says he wants to partner with you on your domestic violence campaign. His daughter was almost killed by her ex-husband and he'd been so thankful to God that she escaped that he has always wanted to do something to help others." Katie put the phone in David's hand and then hugged Gina with a look of astonishment on her face. "I just can't believe this. When I watched that video clip, I thought for sure his deal was done."

"With God, all things are possible, Katie. Even the redemption of a bad boy," Gina told her.

"I guess you're right." She hugged Gina again.

David put the phone to his ear. "Sir, you've got a partner. Let's do something to change this world!"

After everything quieted down, David took the time to admire his new trophy. "You think you're pretty special, don't you?" Gina said as she took the trophy from him.

He pulled Gina close to him. "I am special with you by my side. "I want you in my life, Gina. You and no one else. Once and for all, are you ready for that?"

At that moment, Gina realized that she had been hesitant to go all-in with David because of her experience with Marvel. Gina didn't know if Marvel would ever atone for his sins, but she had just witnessed David lay his misdeeds open for the world to judge, and then he let it be known that it was not okay for any man to put his hands on a woman and make her feel less than what God created her to be. And that was so sexy to Gina. David was altogether different than what she had misjudged him to be. Yes, he had flaws just like everyone else, but he was a good man and she loved him for all that he was and would ever be.

Gina's eyes widened as she realized she'd just admitted to loving David. How it had happened, she didn't know, but it was too late to turn back now. He was her beloved, and she prayed that their love would last a lifetime. "I'm ready my beloved, I'm ready."

The end

Don't forget to join my mailing list:
http://vanessamiller.com/events-join-mailing-list/
Join me on Facebook: https://www.facebook.com/groups/77899021863/
Join me on Twitter: https://www.twitter.com/vanessamiller01

Books in the Loving You Series

Our Love

For Your Love

Got To Be Love

Other Books by Vanessa Miller

Family Business I
Family Business II
Family Business III
Family Business IV
Family Business V
Family Business VI
Our Love
For Your Love
Got To Be Love
Rain in the Promised Land
Heaven Sent
Sunshine And Rain
After the Rain
How Sweet The Sound
Heirs of Rebellion
Feels Like Heaven
Heaven on Earth
The Best of All
Better for Us
Her Good Thing
Long Time Coming
A Promise of Forever Love

A Love for Tomorrow

Yesterday's Promise

Forgotten

Forgiven

Forsaken

Rain for Christmas (Novella)

Through the Storm

Rain Storm

Latter Rain

Abundant Rain

Former Rain

Anthologies (Editor)

Keeping the Faith

Have A Little Faith

This Far by Faith

Novella

Love Isn't Enough

A Mighty Love

The Blessed One (Blessed and Highly Favored series)

The Wild One (Blessed and Highly Favored Series)

The Preacher's Choice (Blessed and Highly Favored Series)

The Politician's Wife (Blessed and Highly Favored Series)

The Playboy's Redemption (Blessed and Highly Favored Series)

Tears Fall at Night (Praise Him Anyhow Series)

Joy Comes in the Morning (Praise Him Anyhow Series)

A Forever Kind of Love (Praise Him Anyhow Series)

Ramsey's Praise (Praise Him Anyhow Series)
Escape to Love (Praise Him Anyhow Series)
Praise For Christmas (Praise Him Anyhow Series)
His Love Walk (Praise Him Anyhow Series)
Could This Be Love (Praise Him Anyhow Series)
Song of Praise (Praise Him Anyhow Series)

For Your Love

Book 2

Loving You Series

by

Vanessa Miller

Prologue

On a cold day in December, Toya Milner was at the hospital with her family. But this time, it was for a joyous occasion. Her younger sister, Tia, had just given birth to a baby girl, Jayden Trinity Carter. She was seven pounds and two ounces of pure beauty, even if she was still all wrinkly and reddish-brown.

Robbie sat on the edge of Tia's bed and held his little girl as if she were some rare, irreplaceable jewel that could break if mishandled. "She's so beautiful. I can't believe this is really our daughter," Robbie said with tears glistening in his eyes.

"Hey, speak for yourself," Tia said. "I am more than capable of making a beautiful child."

The room erupted in laughter. Toya's mother, Pastor Yvonne Milner, was standing next to her co-pastor and Toya's godfather, Thomas Reed. He put his hand on Yvonne's shoulder, and Toya smiled at the sight of them openly displaying affection for each other. They had weathered many storms in the past year, but with the help of the Lord, they had come through it all. Thomas had been patient with her as she'd grown more comfortable with accepting her love for him.

Toya sat in the rocking chair next to the window, waiting for a chance to hold her niece. She smiled at her family, but in truth, Toya wondered when she would have what her mom and Thomas have, or even what Tia and Robbie have. She had been abused by love and wasn't trying to rush back out there, but still, there was something deep inside her that was longing for a love that was true.

Jarrod, Thomas' son, stood behind her. He had been the first man to break her heart, it was only a testament to the God she served that she was able to be friends with him again.

Jarrod poked her arm as he asked, "So if Auntie Yvonne is my godmother, does that make Jayden my god-niece, or what?"

"She could be just your niece if you'd pick up the speed and ask Toya out already," Tia chided him.

Seeing the embarrassed look on Jarrod's face, Yvonne retorted, "Hey, you leave Jarrod alone."

Yeah, leave Jarrod alone, Toya wanted to yell at her sister. The last thing she needed would be for Jarrod to ask her out and not show up again. No, thank you.

Robbie stood up and handed the baby to Toya, then turned back to Tia and cleared his throat. "Tia? I…uh, I'd like to be more to you than just your baby's daddy. I understand why you didn't marry me before, but I have changed. I've been on my job now for over three months and haven't missed a day or gotten written up or anything. I want to be a family. So, what I'm asking is, will you please marry me?"

Tia smiled but then hesitated. "That depends. Will you come to the wedding drunk again?"

"You know I haven't had a thing to drink in months. I'm a Christian now, Tia, and that means something to me. The Lord is helping me to stay sober."

"Well, all right then, Robbie Carter. I guess I'll marry you," Tia said.

The room erupted in cheers. Toya had secretly been rooting for Robbie ever since that night at the hospital when Robbie had refused to leave Tia's side. She'd seen then that the boy had grown into a man—a man well able to take care of his family.

"Okay, why don't we give them some privacy?" Thomas suggested.

After they'd said good-bye to the new parents and baby Jayden, Thomas, Yvonne, Jarrod, and Toya were all about to go to dinner, but Thomas stunned them all when he took hold of Yvonne's hand and slyly grinned. "Well, what about you, Yvonne? Do you think you'll ever marry me?"

"That depends," she said with a hint of mischief in her voice. "Are you going to come to the wedding drunk?"

"Drunk in the spirit and drunk in love? You bet," Thomas answered, then wrapped his arms around her and kissed her tenderly.

When he released her, Yvonne smiled. "Well, in that case, I guess I have no choice but to marry you."

"You always have a choice."

Yvonne shook her head. "I never had a choice, Thomas. You stole my heart, and I don't ever want it back."

"So, it's mine forever?"

"How about... as long as we both shall live?"

Toya glanced over at Jarrod while all this was going on. Her mom and her sister were getting married, but she couldn't seem to find a man... well, there were plenty of men around, but what she needed was a good man.

Jarrod nudged her. "You're next."

Why did he have to say that? She didn't want to hear that from anyone, and especially not the man who provided her with her first broken heart. And she really didn't want to talk about finding love when she was still getting over what happened with Marvel Williams. The man who tricked her into believing he was in love with her, then tried to kill her.

~~~

"Where is the money you promised me?" Clarence Brown asked his partner in crime.

"I don't pay for failed jobs."

"Speak for yourself, Marvel. Because I didn't fail at anything. I practically bankrupted my own church, all you had to do was convince the city to sell you the church. But you were the one who was more interested in destroying Pastor Yvonne and her daughter than making the deal you told me you wanted."

"That's neither here nor there, Brown. I still didn't get what I wanted. And unless you can find out where Toya is, I'm not giving you my money."

"But my wife needs that money. The only reason I got involved with you in the first place was to get her the heart operation she desperately needs."

"Then I suggest you get the information that I desperately need." Marvel hung up and then kicked the trash can next to his desk. Toya and her mother had ruined everything for him. There were warrants out for his arrest, he couldn't run his businesses, and he was stuck in Mexico. But his suffering was nothing compared to what Pastor Yvonne and Toya would soon feel. Revenge was always sweet.

For Your Love
Order your copy today!

About the Author

Vanessa Miller is a best-selling author, entrepreneur, playwright, and motivational speaker. She started writing as a child, spending countless hours either reading or writing poetry, short stories, stage plays and novels. Vanessa's creative endeavors took on new meaning in1994 when she became a Christian. Since then, her writing has been centered on themes of redemption, often focusing on characters facing multi-dimensional struggles.

Vanessa's novels have received rave reviews, with several appearing on *Essence Magazine's* Bestseller's List. Miller's work has receiving numerous awards, including "Best Christian Fiction Mahogany Award" and the "Red Rose Award for Excellence in Christian Fiction." Miller graduated from Capital University with a degree in Organizational Communication. She is an ordained minister in her church, explaining, "God has called me to minister to readers and to help them rediscover their place with the Lord."

She has worked with numerous publishers: Urban Christian, Kimani Romance, Abingdon Press and Whitaker House. She is currently indy published through Praise Unlimited enterprises and working on the Family Business Series.

In 2016, Vanessa launched the Christian Book Lover's Retreat in an effort to bring readers and authors of Christian fiction together in an environment that's all about Faith, Fun & Fellowship. To learn more about Vanessa, please visit her website: www.vanessamiller.com. If you would like to know more about the Christian Book Lover's Retreat that is currently held in Charlotte, NC during the last week in October you can visit: http:// www.christianbookloversretreat.com/index.html

Don't forget to join my mailing list:
http://vanessamiller.com/events/join-mailing-list/
Join me on Facebook: https://www.facebook.com/groups/
77899021863/
Join me on Twitter: https://www.twitter.com/vanessamiller01

CPSIA information can be obtained
at www.ICGtesting.com
Printed in the USA
LVHW030026190821
695524LV00017B/1068